The Coney Island Amateur Psychoanalytic Society and Its Circle

The Coney Island Amateu

Psychoanalytic Society and Its Circle

Aaron Beebe
Zoe Beloff
Amy Herzog
Norman Klein

Edited by Zoe Beloff

NEW YORK
CHRISTINE BURGIN
2009

Luna Park by Moonlight

JOHNNY HEADSTRONG'S

TRIP TO

CLAMS

DRAWINGS BY W. BRUTON

CONEY ISLA

McLOUGHLIN BROS. N.Y.

CONTENTS

Preceding overleaf: Postcard, "Luna Park by Moonlight," 1909.
Opposite: Johnny Headstrong's Trip to Coney Island *by William Bruton, New York: McLoughlin Bros., 1882.*

BARNUM'S MUSEUM

EVERY DAY AND EVENING THIS WEEK,
Ending Saturday, June 3, 1865.

THREE PERFORMANCES DAILY,
MORNING at 11; AFTERNOON at 3; EVENING at 7 3-4.
At morning Performance no extra charge for seats.

MORNING AT 11 O'CLOCK,
BOONE FAMILY COMBINATION,

Consisting of Professor Daniel Boone, aged 9 years, Miss Grace, Miss Myrtle and Miss Lora Gordon Boone, will appear, under the direction of Mrs. Arthur B. Boone.

Lecture, original and amusing...Prof. Daniel Boone
Comic Duett...Misses Grace and Myrtle Boone
Comic Song...Prof. Daniel Boone
Song, "Oh, Loving Heart Trust On," by Gottschalk.............Miss Lora G. Boone
Duett, "The Central Park," by Merton Saxe, Esq...Prof. Dan and Miss Myrtle Boone
Trio, new, "The Boys are Coming Home,"........Misses Lora, Grace and Myrtle Boone
An Address—The Death of our lamented President...............Prof. Dan Boone
Song, "The Cavalier and Shepherdess," by Gottschalk...........Miss Lora G. Boone
Comic Song...Prof. Dan Boone

To be seen at all hours, the most remarkable curiosity in the world,

A HORSE AND RIDER TURNED INTO STONE.

A startling and unparalleled petrifaction, discovered in a cave near the volcano of Chillan, in Buenos Ayres, South America. The Indian and his horse, with an **ENORMOUS SERPENT COILED AROUND THEM**, have evidently all died together—the serpent having crushed the man and horse, and been killed by a poisoned shaft in the death-struggle. The whole fearful group reposing for HUNDREDS OF YEARS in the undisturbed solitude of a damp cave in the South American wilderness, has been gradually covered with limestone accretions dripping from the vault above, and finally, in the course of time, **CONVERTED INTO STONE.**

Lectures upon Mathematics, with Practical Illustrations, by

Prof. HUTCHINGS, LIGHTNING CALCULATOR,

Books which fully teach his system of Calculation, enabling the reader to perform with equal rapidity, may be purchased from Prof. HUTCHINGS. Price 15 cents.

WOODRUFF'S TROUPE OF BOHEMIAN GLASS BLOWERS,

Who will exhibit without extra charge, in WAX FIGURE HALL,

A GLASS STEAM ENGINE

In full operation. They also manufacture an endless variety of charming ornaments.

A Mammoth Fat Woman,

MISS ROSINA D. RICHARDSON, WEIGHING 660 lbs.

EXTRAORDINARY FEMALE SPECIMEN OF A NEW RACE FROM CIRCASSIA.

MISS ANNA SWAN, NOVA SCOTIA GIANTESS,
EIGHT FEET ONE INCH HIGH!!!

A MENAGERIE OF LIVING ANIMALS,

THE CELEBRATED BENHAM HOG

The largest in the world, weighing when alive, 1,335 pounds.

PHRENOLOGICAL EXAMINATIONS in Ten Minutes, by
PROF. LIVINGSTON.

The Curiosity Shop,

On Second Floor of the Museum, contains several rare and curious articles, not to be obtained elsewhere—mementoes of a visit to the Museum.

GRAND AQUARIA, OCEAN and RIVER GARDENS, MINIATURE SKATING POND, ALBINO BOY, LIVING OTTERS, ENORMOUS SERPENTS, LEARNED SEAL NED, & LIVING HAPPY FAMILY! Birds and Animals of diverse natures, living in peace and harmony!

Visitors will find the ILLUSTRATED MUSEUM GUIDE BOOK at the door and at the refreshment stands, for the bare cost of printing, 15 cents.
PHOTOGRAPH CARTES DE VISITE of the principal Curiosities, are furnished to visitors as KEEPSAKES, at the low price of 15 cents each.

MADAME LA COMPTE,

SOOTHSAYER and ASTROLOGIST, niece to the celebrated M'lle Le Normand, adviser to Napoleon I., may be consulted at all hours.

Barnum's Curiosity Engraving,

Will be presented to each visitor, on condition that it shall be posted in some safe and conspicuous place in the town where such visitor resides. To be had at the door.

The Elegant Prismatic Light,
IN THE FORM OF A BRILLIANT STAR,

Erected on the Museum Front, was imported by E. DE FRIES, 638 Broadway.

Admittance to all, only 30 cts.........Children under 10 years.........15 cts.
Reserved Seats in Parquette and Balcony...................................30 cts. extra
Single Seats in Private Boxes...60 cts. extra
Entire Private Boxes...5 dollars extra

THE CONEY ISLAND MUSEUM

A Brief History of the Way Things
That Weren't Separate Are Separate Now

Aaron Beebe, Director

Coney Island means a lot of things to a lot of people. In its heyday, it represented the best elements of American Modernity and the spirit of invention and entrepreneurism writ large. Preserving and furthering those ideals is a business enterprise and an institutional challenge in itself. The Coney Island Museum is the only museum in the world dedicated to the culture and history of Coney Island, home of the world's first enclosed amusement parks and an epicenter of American culture. The oldest items in the museum's collection date to the late nineteenth century, but the museum's story starts a great deal earlier. Like all museums, its roots lie in the eighteenth and nineteenth centuries, during a convergence of some aspects of our culture that seem very distinct today, when the boundaries between categories we now take for granted, between "high and low," "art and science," "education and entertainment," were not as clear as they are now.

The story of that convergence and its glorious climax in Coney Island begins in the 1700s, when enlightenment thinking gave rise to an institution called "the arts and sciences." It pursued a doctrine of curiosity and observation and recognized that if one looked closely enough at any aspect of the world, documented it, and thought hard about what one had seen or drawn, it could be understood. This included any subject, from nature to architecture, theater, art, and history. The key words were *wonder* and *curiosity*, and it eventually became a philosophy that was open to any- and everyone. Over time, small business owners, statesmen, and

Opposite: Broadside for Barnum's Museum, week ending June 3, 1865. When someone asked P. T. Barnum if one of his exhibits was "real," he replied, "Persons who pay their money at the door have the right to form their own opinions after they have gone upstairs."

CEOs increasingly doubled as inventors and showmen. By the 1800s there was a flurry of public experimentation with science, commerce, and knowledge seeking as multidisciplinary institutions devoted to fulfilling these concepts popped up everywhere. Benjamin Franklin, P. T. Barnum, and Thomas Edison were all products of this ideology, and it led to the creation of both Barnum's Museum and the American Museum of Natural History. These were living institutions combining live entertainment, art, and history under one roof. The peak moment for these fruitful experiments was at the beginning of the twentieth century, when advances in the realm of automated technology, mechanization, and electricity became a part of the mix and Coney Island produced the world's first amusement parks.

Coney Island in those years represented the apex of these arts and science ideals. With its three amusement parks and myriad smaller attractions, it was Barnum's Museum on a grand scale—and in its combination of the spectacle of world's fairs, the visionary inventiveness of American entrepreneurial ingenuity, and the brutality and closed-mindedness of colonial might, it was unlike anything the world had ever seen. There on the beach, one could find small theaters and wax museums; business owners fought for customers through innovation and entertainment; even the amusement parks had their own theater companies. Inside the parks and out, visitors could see large-scale reenactments of events that had happened on the other side of the world; they could experience scientific advances that they'd only dreamed about and could exercise their curiosity and sense of wonder and overcome their skepticism—if only for a few hours. All these elements were promoted equally. It was handmade and huge, and its sideshows and midways were a destination for the thrill seeker, the workingman, and the visiting dignitary alike.

But finally, after all that buildup, ten years or so into the new millennium, it was all over. Coney Island continued to thrive, but those institutions founded on the premise that wonderment led to discovery moved on. The twentieth century was marked by a widening distinction between the arts and sciences. Disciplines specialized and became rarified. Businessmen ceased to be entertainers or inventors. The museum and the sideshow—once siblings or partners—moved apart and disavowed each other as it became more important to be correct than to be intrigued. The rubes went one way and the eggheads another.

Today, only a shadow of that earlier time survives. But there is change again in the air. A hundred years on, it is artists who are continuing the tradition of exploration and observation, following in the footsteps of those who built Coney Island. With an eye toward undoing the split between fact and fantasy, art and science, they are beginning to break down the disciplinary boundaries that have come to separate them from "the hard sciences." In many cases, they are even creating their work from inside laboratories and academic departments. Biotechnology, anthropology, psychology, history: these are the fields of art in 2009. Like Coney Island a hundred years ago, the art world is combining observation and excitement with theater, architecture, and visual art, presenting them to eager audiences in new and entrepreneurial ways.

The Coney Island Museum strives to emulate the living museums of the nineteenth century by combining live entertainment, art, and history in ways that highlight their similarities rather than their differences. Exhibitions become a means of blurring counterproductive boundaries and of asking new questions about the role that Coney Island plays in the world today as well as throughout its history. By bringing artists into the museum and giving them unlimited access to the collection, the museum is encouraging artists to speak history with their own voice; to pull stories from the pieces of Coney Island's past and tell them in ways that defy boundaries and explore the possibilities inherent in both Coney Island and in the museum itself. Like the incubator shows that graced the halls of Luna Park for more than forty years, these exhibitions can be at one and the same time educational, life saving, prurient, and obscene.

Artists are the inventors of our age and it's their vision that will keep Coney Island a place full of fresh ideas and wondrous spectacles. Harnessing that vision, Coney Island can become the center of a new kind of amusement and a place where the rift between the museum and the carnivalesque past is healed. It can once again be the center of a cluster of attractions the likes of which the world has never seen, filled with objects of wonder and enthusiasm, shock and surprise. By letting go of the constraints of skepticism and isolation, we can pay tribute to the minds that brought us Coney Island in the first place while encouraging those that will continue to enrich it in the future.

pages 12–13: "Shoot the Chutes," Luna Park, photographed by the Noyes family, 1904.
pages 14–15: Drawing for shooting gallery target by William F. Mangels (1866–1958),
W. F. Mangels Co. Carousell Works, Coney Island, ca. 1918–19.
pages 16–17: "Crazy Town," Luna Park, Coney Island, 1913.

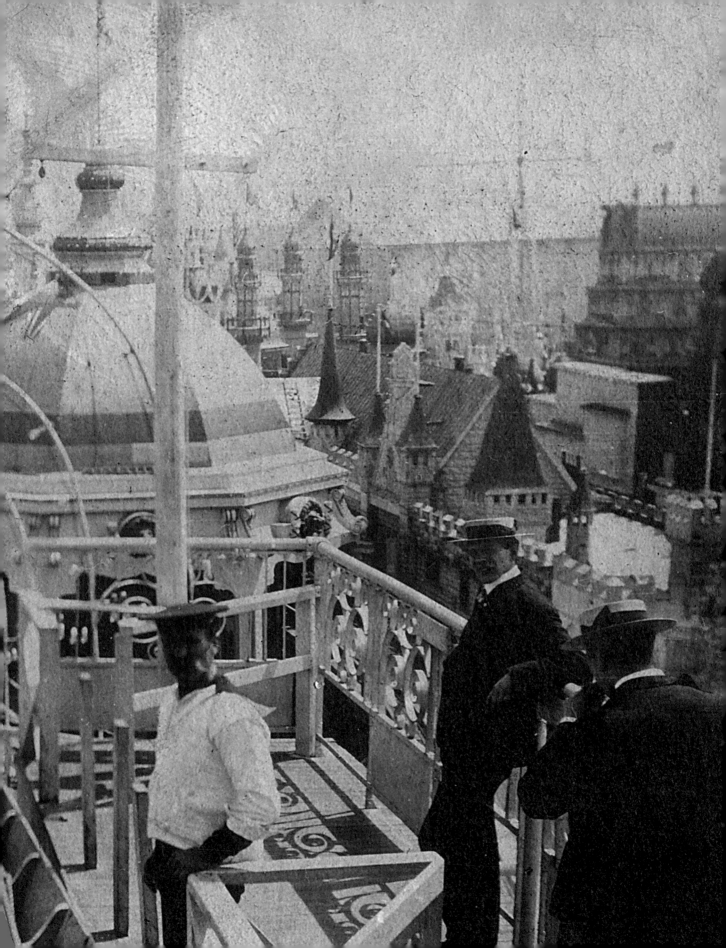

3 Ft.

12 Ft.

LUNA PARK, CONEY ISL'D

Coney   Island N.Y.
        August 3I st/09.
Having the time of our lives.
                Ma.

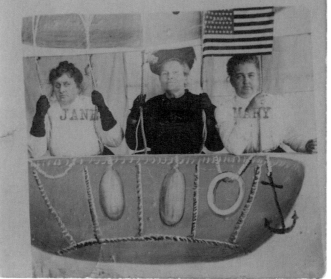

FREUD IN CONEY ISLAND

Norman M. Klein

The facts are simple enough: in September 1909 a relatively unknown
Freud spent a week in New York City, en route to a lecture series
upstate at Clark University. The air ranged from muggy to stifling. The
museum exhibition on antiquities, the one he had high hopes for, proved
substandard. The crowds on the street smelled of industrial fluids and
sweat. Even friendly faces made him squirm. The conductor on a tram
tried to be empathetic: he ordered the crowd to make room for "the old
man." But Freud did not see himself as old, not yet. He pulled back his
shoulders and glared, then felt idiotic.

Back in the hotel, his stomach was churning from American food.
His mouth tasted like rancid milk. His neck felt numb. I'm truly a mass
of symptoms, he told himself. I'm a neurasthenic woman. I'll wake up
paralyzed on my left side. I need a day by the sea. He rummaged through
his trunk for a lighter suit. In the morning, before the sewer vapors hit
the sidewalks once again, he took a ferry to Coney Island. Of course
increasingly, as we know now, he kept these anxieties—his own case
study—in separate leather notebooks, a psychiatric form of double
book-keeping.

As the boat chugged along, smoke from Manhattan evaporated into
blue mist. Finally the ferry anchored at Dreamland Pier (what someone
called Old Iron Pier). A friendly gust of sea air greeted him, but the view
made him wince, like architectural gastritis. A lunatic tower dominated,
built like a hodgepodge—vaguely Moorish on top, wedding-cake Venetian
in the middle, a wigwam at the bottom. Clustered around it were buildings
so tentative, so flimsy, they could have been built with eggshells; they
were sketches in pasteboard. Then, toward the horizon, he saw streets that
looked like the day after mardi gras, like a gigantic drunken operetta.

Opposite: Real Photo Postcard, Coney Island, August 31, 1909.

Luckily it was still early in the morning. Even the mist had not yet burned off. The main streets, Surf Avenue and the Bowery, looked sleepy. But then the turmoil began. Within an hour, they were already jammed with confusion. Armies seemed to be scattering in retreat. Freud tried to hide on the beach but after a few hours decided to enter the "irresponsible gaiety." He started taking notes in one of those leather journals that would remain hidden, even from many friends and admirers, for ninety years.

At the entrance to Luna Park, he noticed two monkeys on a chain, mother and child. The mother was baring her teeth and hissing while a crowd poked at her little boy, some with umbrellas, canes, some with their index fingers. The monkey child's movements utterly reminded him of children he had treated, a monkey Little Hans. If this were an infant, a shock this fierce would undoubtedly lead to phobic behavior. What if monkeys stored this shock in an early mental place, a primal sod? And what if this atavistic place survived while the species evolved—like gills or tailbones inside the fetus? It would lie hidden below more intricate formations. And yet it would still operate as a mechanism, perhaps fainter in humans than monkeys; or even more convoluted, like folds on the brain. Surely there would be no therapeutic way to find a psychic spot so ancient.

The monkey child under attack stared agonistically, almost christlike. Freud tried to interpret its sublunar gaze, but its eyes were a deep onyx. He managed to capture this thought in only a single sentence, beneath complaints about the boiled sausage he had just eaten.

There is reason to believe that Freud walked into Dreamland, the last and most bourgeois of the three amusement parks in Coney Island. To enter, one had to pass through "Creation," a music-hall version of Genesis. Creation began at the mouth of a huge tunnel, featuring the massive thighs and vagina of a plaster nude thirty feet high. Her breasts were larger than haystacks. She sparked at least two sentences. A phrase from one survives, in the recently uncovered Freud Ephemera: "…or do Americans prefer genitalia large enough to crush a man, or at least ruin his hat?" As many scholars have noted since the Freud Ephemera turned up in London (1999), biblical fantasy was highly eroticized in Coney Island or turned into a circus freak show, with little boys as Mephistopheleses selling bags of peanuts, and dwarves with their own freak town.

We are also reasonably certain that Freud went to Hell—not only the Hell Gate in Dreamland, but also Darkness and Dawn (with Hell as

Darkness) in Luna Park. He enjoyed watching the Chicago Fire (with women jumping from flaming windows). Nearby he claimed his hair was nearly singed when the riverboat *Prairie Belle* burst into flames along the Mississippi. He even yawned his way down "Stygian chambers," to the River Styx, and saw the Flood at the Crack of Dawn.

Hell Gate at Dreamland caught his attention most of all, particularly its shoddy construction and miserable ventilation. The fires of the damned were made of crêpe paper. The walls of Hell were papier-mâché. A reasonable Flood from God could have dissolved it all in five minutes. But the mood in Hell had a "strangeness and irresponsible gaiety" that Freud assumed was an American problem. Americans like cheerful torture, he decided. Fairy-tale rape, Jung would probably call it (Jung would have a field day with all this). "Americans will take a long trolley ride just to pretend to be buried alive. They think being molested by circus freaks is the most uncanny (*unheimlich*) thing of all."

A pretty red-haired girl caught Freud's eye as she wandered into Hell Gate. A girl of twenty, she adjusted her new bonnet, posed cheerfully in the mirror. Suddenly, demons in cheap tights grabbed her. With a look of supreme boredom, they lifted her by her armpits. The more she kicked and cursed, the harder they laughed. Then they dumped her like a dead cat down a long trough. Her taffeta undergarment rustled while she skidded out of sight. Afterward, the demons turned and cackled mindlessly for the crowd. An exhausted, obviously gin-soaked Satan snickered his approval. This stale laughter was supposed to be infectious.

Meanwhile, the young lady's screams faded away. In like manner, her sliding body seemed to hit bottom. Freud heard a faint thud. But then two minutes later, she came storming back. Angrily, she planted her new hat (a tuque or toque) back on her head. Then she gestured rudely, "in a masculine way," at the demons and Satan. Puffing up, she looked ready to slap someone, but then inexplicably did not. Instead she broke into a smile. After all, Freud wrote, she had just paid at least ten cents to be there. Within twenty minutes, eleven more well-dressed women were thrown down one hole or another, with barely a peep from any of them, like Dover soles being boned and dressed. But that was not the only indignity women had to suffer "with a smile." At the Luna Park next door, many well-appointed ladies, even ladies of a certain age, were shoved on top of a small hole where a powerful gust of air blew their dresses above their thighs. Then everyone was supposed to whoop it up. Thank goodness my wife and daughter are back in Vienna, Freud noted. Imagine them disappearing like shit down a hole, with their thighs exposed. A newspaper he found called this "a nightmare world that claims to be bizarre and fantastic."

In German, Freud detailed a sermon given at Hell Gate, to justify everything he had seen. A wholesome preacher approached like a sturdy tenor ("the face of a farmer, the look of a swindler"). Men should not squeeze unmarried women, the preacher declared. Nor should women "outcasts" steal from drunken men. In fact, all whiskey and beer "arouses the passions." But most of all, one must keep Satan from his door: be sure to pay your preachers as much as you can afford. Then Freud heard the ceiling begin to ache. He looked up. It was barely supporting a fat archangel sliding on a wire. Satan gasped loudly, then went into bad pantomime. He howled like a man screaming on cue, then dived down a pit.

Afterward, Freud lingered in Hell for at least twenty minutes more. Then two demons came by. They warned him to stop writing, then began to cackle and head in his direction. So he left in a hurry. But there lies the scholarly problem: how did Freud understand the sermon in English? Clearly by then he had been joined by a friend of Sàndor Ferenczi, probably two friends. It appears that Ferenczi was too busy setting up the lecture series, so he sent these two unlikely people in his stead. They were his former patients, "success stories that proved the genius of psychoanalysis." What's more, they knew Coney Island all too well and spoke German and Yiddish. First there was a pretty woman in her early thirties, with a full face and large brooding eyes. Like a parody of a therapist, she tended to her high-strung cousin, a man with the same deeply sunken eyes and a peculiar scar from his earlobe down to his jaw.

Guiding Freud back to Surf Avenue, they paid ten cents to have his picture taken (not the faked photograph so often assumed to be Freud, but the photo in Folio 7 of the Ephemera). Here we see Freud in a cloud of confusion, fighting for his dignity. We literally see him looking up with suspicion. He was getting hints of what he was up against. Then the facts were made plain: the man, named Al, was haunted by the unspent yearnings of a dead relative. He felt "her" crawling inside his chest, whispering to him. Over the years, she had "forced" him into horrible business investments that wasted the family fortune. "She" (or it) had also coaxed Al into chilly love affairs with dull women that "she" found acceptable. But to Al, they were invariably too scrawny, too squinty, too withdrawn.

However, lately Al had stopped feeling haunted. Thanks to Frida, he was now applying Ferenczi's collective hypnosis to silence the dead relative. By contrast, only three months ago this dead voice—whose name could not be spoken out loud, not even written down—had forced Al to hear the pumping of blood throughout his body. "Dead Relative" (as he called her) had sensed a constriction somewhere. She warned Al that he was due for a massive heart attack. Al fell into a panic. He listened sleeplessly to the burbling of his arteries, until at last he went into false angina and found himself in the hospital.

But nothing like that invaded this cheerful late afternoon (not yet). Al was doing "fine, feeling chipper." With Al doing so well, Freud shifted his attention elsewhere. He noticed that Frida had immensely long eyelashes. Surely behind those eyes she had serious reaction formations as well, he thought. Why else would she devote herself like a sister of mercy to Al? He clearly was not available, not for romance, not even for much conversation—"not this year," she said, rather pointedly.

The two cousins (or was that three, with Dead Relative in hiding?) ushered Freud to a bath house near Steeplechase Park. They translated in English for Freud. His throat was parched. They got him a frozen ice. Then with a loud sigh, Freud plumped onto a rented steam chair and nodded off instantly. However, as Folio 7.6 indicates, he then slipped into rather frantic dreams. At the height of his busy sleep, he saw Frida staring at him. Her immense eyes were floating or ticking like a clock. Her stare awoke him with a start. He sat bolt upright, in a sweat. There indeed was Frida looming over him. She had been studying him and gathering her thoughts.

Through Ferenczi (his reverent disciple, at least in 1909), she had been absorbing Freud's newest book about Little Hans, the five-year-old phobic boy, and also the recent case study of the Rat Man, about *zwangsneurose*, obsessive-compulsive neurosis. (She was only beginning to internalize his Wolf Man essay.) And now, as if by miracle, less than a week after she had returned home, the author himself was having troubled dreams before her, twisting and turning right there in the flesh. It was only weeks since her self-hypnosis with Ferenczi (and Al) had undergone that famous breakthrough (cited in Gottlieb et al.). There Freud was, supine, still dapper at fifty-three, hair only faintly gray, though a little matted from all he had been through. Just seeing him sparked insights. But she had learned through bitter experience that when you speak to bright men, you must frame your words very slowly and tilt your head toward the light. We only have the gist of what she said, though it went on for some time. First she posed a question (while posing, so to speak):

"Suppose reaction formations are driven by erotic denial?"

Freud answered: "Yes, they are."

"Well then," she went on, "can reaction formations act on groups? That is, the same as it affects people alone?"

"Perhaps," Freud answered, then thought again. "Yes, of course.... It must."

"Well (stretching her neck for a moment, pausing to catch the light)...that means a group plays by the same emotional rules as a person alone. Basically?"

The late afternoon cast a spell over her face. She smiled and reworded her question: "Put it another way. Let's take the crowd at Hell Gate. Does their phobic play work the same as Little Hans by himself?"

Freud stared at her with renewed interest. Sensing his approval, she ranted on about Coney Island attractions for ten minutes or more. Freud particularly remembered her description of men who loved being zapped by electrical prods in Luna Park. Then he noticed that her palm was moist when she squeezed his hand. Her eyes transformed from hazel to coral in the late afternoon light. But even worse, her mouth reminded him of Sabina Spielrein, the patient with the sway in her walk. Freud knew that she was already Jung's mistress. Jung, that *kuppler* (pimp), had even coaxed her to write to Freud, asking him to mop up the affair. Jung sent her to Freud like a taste of meat left on the bone, to show off the line of her face, the slim neck.

The sun burned into the ocean, leaving Frida in silhouette. Freud shifted his head, and like an optical illusion, Sabina's face substituted for Frida.

As Freudian scholars know, this was not the first time that he underwent this phenomenon; simply the most haunting, the most cited in the Ephemera. Facial transpositions often bothered Freud. Usually, they came during the third or fourth year of extensive therapy. Frida had simply jumped a few steps ahead. Freud often compared these transpositions to phosphenes caused by the sun. "A husband transposes his mother's face onto his wife's naked body," he wrote in 1916, then crossed it out.

As R. R. Greenblatt pointed out at the groundbreaking conference on the Ephemera (2002), "Freud tried to live above or below the erotic fixations that he discussed." Frida's answer was even simpler. To her, Coney Island was a psychiatric teeter-totter. Reality keeps uneasy company with pleasure, she said. The outside pretends to have collective sex with the inside.

Freud answered with a sociological theory. "The lower classes in Coney Island are not as sexually repressed as the cultured classes," he declared, his voice rising. Case closed. He slammed his notebook, to emphasize—punctuate—when something from outside floated toward him. He sensed a ripple of hysteria fifty yards away. Al was spinning like a dervish, his arms splayed outward as he turned. A crowd of beer drinkers formed a circle to watch. Al became an attraction. He had just seen a dwarf on Surf Avenue who completely, I mean utterly, resembled the Dead Relative. Suddenly, the weather turned gloomy around him. Voices came at him. Four of these voices felt like winds landing on his head, making the shape of a cross. Next, Al heard music that sounded like insects climbing into his ears, making him dizzy with vertigo. Frida was heart struck. Freud had to serve as the doctor in the house. Two hours passed (no notes). But clearly the day went from bad to much worse.

Sometime after eight Jung may have arrived, and Ferenczi, they say. That is, of course, what biographies have told us, that they cruised and schmoozed together, a genteel evening by the sea. But now we know that Freud asked his friends, particularly Jung and Ferenczi, to hide events of his day in Coney Island. I am not convinced why. It was not simply those two patients. Al's episode, his catalytic ferment, as Ferenczi called it, should not have overwhelmed Freud. No doubt something larger convinced everyone to maintain silence for the rest of their lives. Even Ernest Jones was kept out of the loop.

Now, however, the Ephemera restores part of that day, though not enough. We are still left to fill in the blanks. At least two hours are missing, perhaps even twelve, from morning through night. Frida brought Freud back to his hotel. Something may have happened that night or the next day. Five years later, Frida married a career officer in the German army, but by 1920 she had disappeared. Al meanwhile slogged along for decades, lived an astonishing long life on vapors, like bacteria living on a rock. He died as haunted as ever, but with a heart going as strong as a furnace, at the ripe age of seventy-four. His brain simply gave way, but he never had a cold in his life. Paranoia kept him fresh.

Now we return to that week in New York. Standard documents leave us only a few dyspeptic facts: soon after visiting Coney Island, both Freud and Jung suffered diarrhea, each on different days. New York food troubled them. That is well established. Also, on the Wednesday after Coney Island, Freud went to Columbia University, where he involuntarily urinated down his pants, left a mortally embarrassing stain. He and Jung discussed whether he should enter therapy for the problem. And sometime that year, once if not twice, he and Jung plunged into one of their fiercest oedipal arguments, only partially about Sabina, mostly about the paranormal. As their rage steamed the wallpaper off the walls, Freud simply fainted; he hyperventilated or fell very briefly into grief at the loss of his "adoptive" son. No wonder he called America a land of savages.

By 1914 Sabina was replaced by Toni Wolff as Jung's mistress, as a permanent "aunt" for his children. Jung in turn hinted that Freud had sex with Sabina. Freud exploded. That was the end of their dysfunctional family. Now the Ephemera answers some of the nagging questions, about Ferenczi's private adventures as well.

Right before transmogrifying in front of Freud that day, Frida had gone back to Hungary for six months to be treated by Ferenczi. There she met a married man of limited potential named Moscowitz, who changed his name to Klein in order to dance as a gentile in the Austrian empire—mostly to get away from his wife, the farm, the goats, the gristmill, the cheese. "M+K," as Ferenczi calls him in his notes, had a stepsister in Budapest who was something of a panderer. She ran a rooming house in Budapest that often rented to women of an "uncertain reputation." Ferenczi warned Frida against staying there, but Al seemed to be less haunted around prostitutes. That made the day, at least, much easier for Frida. So she left Al there, while she stayed with M+K. But every night she returned to the rooming house to drag Al back to earth and take him to the music hall. There M+K performed what one reviewer called the worst dance act in Budapest. But M+K was indefatigably cheerful, a relief from Al. That allowed Frida to be loyal to all the men in her life. After the show, she could walk Al back to the rooming house. There Al met his favorite, a young Polish girl whose pubic hair was very red, like a fox in a burrow, he used to say. Afterward, Frida pretended to sway in rhythm to M+K flying high beside her, reenacting his czardas as they wandered home.

Finally, after a few months, M+K took a train back to his village, near what is now the Slovakian border. His son's wife was about to give birth to his grandson, who would be known as Young Yussell, a Yiddish nickname for the Hebrew name for Jesus. But Young Yussell was hardly a Jesus, certainly not a mystic, even when ghosts crossed his path. For example, when he was ten, in the chaos after the Great War, Young Yussell finished tending the goats as the sun went down, and he walked to a clearing in the woods near the farm. There he saw an old table thirty feet long. The surface had been carved with an adze hundreds of years ago. The table was piled with roasted meats. Dozens of revelers were eating loudly. They were dressed in what Yussell called "very old clothing." When asked what he meant, he answered, "older than anyone wears anymore." They wore tights and codpieces. Some had feathered hats. The leather of their shoes and shirts was tanned in the old way. They were from another century.

He walked up to the table, and it disappeared. With the table gone, he could see the clearing through the moonlight back to the farm. Yussell never wondered what had taken place. Why question?, he asked. Did the ghosts leave any food for me? Yussell believed the earth was no rounder than you could walk in a day. It was flat because your shoes were flat. It was no more haunted than bugs on your food or a smell where you sat.

But through Frida, Yussell's ghost story finally came to Ferenczi's attention. He used it as ammunition against Freud's argument about the insoluble nature of the unconscious. Freud answered in this way:

A man who feels a great thirst at night after enjoying highly seasoned food for supper often dreams that he is drinking. Of course the dream never satisfies a strong desire for food or drink. Young Yussell had probably missed supper. But even as a boy, he knew that you cannot quench your thirst by dreaming. From such a dream, one awakes thirsty, and the hallucination dries up in the moonlight. That is your folklore for you, your haunted forest.

For example, in 1913, Freud complained of patients who dreamt in fairy tales, conjuring up Rumpilstiltskin and so on. He decided that they were satisfying a wish fulfillment, but not out of collective folk memory. Instead, they were dreaming of moments from their childhood nursery (screen memory). A patient dreams of a copy of Doré's illustrations to *Perrault's Fairy Tales* (1867). One image haunts him, is engrammed in his memory, of Little Red Riding Hood lying in bed beside the wolf. She stares ahead in dreamy anticipation. The Wolf's great snout is almost handsome, very carefully modeled. In the end, it remained clear to Freud that neither folktales nor popular illustrations nor Coney Island—nor a visit to the Acropolis nor the Loch Ness monster—could generate dream work, not in the way that the id (the primal I) did.

Something like narcissism, depersonalization, or infantile regression might generate Yussell's brief identity crisis. These were hallucinatory flashes, again like Freud at the Acropolis, but nothing on the order of what we find in Freud's notebooks about Coney Island (discussed variously in Folios 7–9). When the codex of the Ephemera finally appears (2005), the public will see what a few scholars have confronted since its discovery in 1999. Readers will have to take the same journey. It turns out that his day in Coney Island extends for another eighty years at least. It echoes throughout the twentieth century, easily from 1909 to 1989, even to 2004.

We return to that day for more clues. In 1918, he writes:

From the boardwalk, I saw women in bustles and women in stone, but not stone. It was a warm day, as warm as the Prater on a Sunday in summer. I remember New York from the boardwalk, and have hidden what it suggested about some of my work. I do not suppose anyone will need to know about my casual impressions of Coney Island in 1908.

We know, of course, that the boardwalk was not formally installed in Coney Island until 1920, not all seven miles from the parks to Sea Gate. Only the Bowery remained as part of an earlier boardwalk. Freud even mistakenly dates his visit to "the American Prater" as 1908, as if the crises with Jung in 1909 had not happened yet. But most of all, clearly the elegance of the Prater was hardly the same as the roaring half-mile of the Bowery boardwalk. Consider this description in 1908:

Busy blocks—eating booths, hot frankfurters on the grill, beef dripping on the spit, wash-boilers of green corn steaming in the center of hungry groups who gnawed on [them] as if playing harmonicas; photograph galleries, the sitters ghastly in the charnel-house glare…open-faced moving picture shows [that] invite effrontery from the jocose crowd; chop suey joints, fez-topped palmists, strength tests; dance halls and continuous song-and-dance entertainments; girls…in tights and spangles (except on the Sabbath). Bands, orchestras, pianos at war with gramophones, hand-organs, calliopes; overhead, a roar of wheels in a death lock with shrieks and screams; whistles, gongs, rifles all busy; the smell of candy, popcorn, meats, beer, tobacco, blended with the odor of the crowd redolent now and then of patchouli; a steaming river of people, arches over by electric signs—this is the Bowery at Coney Island.

We also know that Freud saw his first moving pictures that week, possibly at Coney Island; and was again singularly unimpressed, like the classic statement by Kafka a few years later, that movies were only "iron shutters" that disturb one's vision, forcing the eye to jump from one vision to another, "putting the eye into uniform." (We know, of course, that Freud always compared his day in Coney Island to the hounds of world war.) It was indeed so difficult for turn-of-the-century modernists (Freud, Kafka, Bergson), who were shaped before mass entertainment took charge, to perceive its imagery as more than the sweat of the crowd.

Anyway, by 1928, Freud had completed his meta-theory about Coney Island as a "sidelong glance" in notes about group dynamics, transference neurosis, the psychopathology of everyday life, lay analysis, taboo systems. But the crisis was not laid to rest, not even as displacement, particularly after the war. Freud even mentally returned to Coney Island (Folio 9) as he labored over his answer to Rousseau, *Civilization and Its Discontents*. But even there, the phobic play of the crowds in Coney Island had to remain scrupulously outside of his system. "I have invented a map like a wall brick by brick," he writes. "But the exception makes the map," he added. Thus, in the Ephemera, the Coney Island material defines what he calls *abseits liegend*, "outlying." It was basic to the place that could not be mapped into his topology, even at the end of his life, particularly by the end (as in references to the hounds of war as a thrill ride). We see Freud dying of cancer of the jaw on the eve of the Second World War. One of his final notes refers to a dark Coney Island–like hallucination. As the pain and the opium ripen together, he describes "the spiral dream," where "phobic play" converts into spiraling machines crushing his Europe.

Of course, 1928 became another milestone, we now know. However, why a milestone still remains unclear. We are forced one more time into guess work. What was so riveting to Freud about this particular "surprise" in 1928? That is, after so many other surprises appear as cryptographic references in the Ephemera, what Greenblatt calls "his secret language to himself as a twin." All we know is that for perhaps the twentieth time from 1905 to 1928, Freud withheld what he called a "surprise." He isolated it from his public record. Even in Folio 9, he reveals only enough for him to remember. As he wrote in the Addendum: "To know that you will be plundered (*da wirst geplundert*) like a ruin for a thousand years is to be haunted by the future." At any rate, this "surprise" of 1928 (he called it *überraselung*, an oddly antique word) apparently required special handling. It was a last straw of some kind, an event he kept from his family as well. Freud had to change the diaries as a result, make a structural revision. In the summer of 1928 he gathered the leather Folios 7–9, then added 1–8, and converted them into a secret incunabula of sorts. Each volume was fitted in its box (so often compared to a cigar box). And within each box, he also inserted the famous "lost" photos, sketches, and other ephemera (thus the name). All nine boxes were then joined like a piece of crude marquetry inside a larger case, something built for him that could be locked up.

This case traveled with Freud when he left his apartment for London in 1937. He described it once as "the relic of a family pet." For the crossing to London, it was wrapped in a blanket and stored inside a steamer trunk. A year later, as his illness worsened, he planned for the future of his incunabula. He set up the unknown last requests. And they were observed to the letter, as far as we know. Finally, even the requests themselves were permanently lost, when the family servant entrusted with them died in 1954. Not until 1999 did the waterlogged wooden crate finally turn up. At first it was catalogued and auctioned off, as "a handmade typewriter case filled with travel diaries by an Austrian physician, circa 1920."

But let us return to another key event from 1928: Freud's meetings with Soviet artist/designer El Lissitzky. They already knew each other, perhaps as early as 1922, but only casually. In the fall of 1928, however, they met for days. We imagine the two international Jews struggling over a coffee at first, trying to find a common interest, a common humanity. They politely disagree about America, about its potential. Freud drops hints about strange notes on America (*fremdheit*), private scribblings, not a part of his public lectures.

"I have often wondered," Freud said, "if the shape of Coney Island parks resembles my model of the mind. By that I mean, does real space reproduce unconscious space?"

Lissitzky, the former architect, the constructivist spatial designer (PROUNs), was thrilled by the concept. Was there a way, beyond the ghoulish cuteness of amusement parks, to build a space where the symptoms and formations of Freud's theories could be acted out—to walk around Freud's model as if at a theater, or in a cathedral, or on a city boulevard?

Freud and Lissitzky began to imagine what shape this phantasmagoria should assume (*Trugbild, Wahngebilde*). Freud's version suggested an inveterate Viennese on a long walk inside the Ring. He kept returning to the layer-cake design of Viennese housing, with its half floor above the store level—that would be a preconscious—followed by cathectic, aseptic layers above. The boiler in the basement he saw as a kind of *ich* or id. It radiated heat like "vengeance rising through the floorboards." A roof leaking cathected from overhead, also like the id: "to be invaded by pent-up weather is a dream of drowning in your parents' embrace."

Lissitzky preferred something more functional, yet whimsical, like his Lenin's lecture tower, a much more open floor plan for the unconscious. Instead of Freud's sketch of the unconscious in only two tiers above ground (one for childhood shock, one for adult neurosis), Lissitzky needed something more imbricated. One day he brought Sabbatini's old manual from 1638, about how to build illusions in the theater; for example, how to turn a man into a stone and back again.

Inside Sabbatini, he found evidence explaining Freud's quote about the Prater. When it came to architecture, Freud preferred a soothing unconscious, where humans and motorized statues from their life (like an amusement park) cohabitated in Baroque elegance, like Descartes' fascination with automatons designed as a singing lake. But Lissitzky's maquette included motorized walls and ceilings as well, an "ideogrammatic machine." His "cine-collage" model even influenced Eisenstein for a few months (generating a brief film by Eisenstein, now lost—about two minutes long). But Lissitzky's package never returned to the Soviet Union. With the coming of the first five-year plan, and with the momentous suicide of Mayakovsky, Lissitzky decided to leave his Freud/PROUN in Germany. He built a small, motorized journey zigzagging on a hydraulic stage, filled with electromagnetic puppets and sliding involutions, like cilia or a Coney Island mystery ride, to reenact cathexis in a Freudian space; along with vectors of water forming psycho-ideograms on sheets of glass against one wall, that was also incised with names that Freud wrote especially for the project, including Dreamland and Hell Gate.

Lissitzky's design, with Freud's commentary, was stored in a basement in Bremen. There they hibernated until 1966, when the architect Sándor

Hartobagi found them. Behind a sketch on wood, Hartobagi peeled away three pages, sticky from moisture, and a rusty, warped model. Most of the text had been eaten away by fungus, like a Dead Sea scroll. A signature indicated someone called "Ds. Df." Even Hartobagi guessed that it was an inversion of s..igmund f…reud. However, not until 1999 was the handwriting verified as Freud's; along with more on Freud/PROUN found in Folio 9 of the Ephemera.

Why so long for this discovery to emerge? Hartobagi's brief essay, with architectural charts, came out only in Hungarian (a language not widely read), so Freud/PROUN disappeared once again. However, it survived as urban legend for young architects in prewar Vienna, particularly for Victor Gruen. Finally, after the shocks of the war, in 1956, the émigré Gruen made his mark in the U.S. He completed the first of his many multilevel enclosed malls, the Southdale Shopping Center in the Edina suburb of Minneapolis. At the historic opening, after three vodka martinis and no sleep for two days, Gruen made a slip of the tongue, a parapraxis. Freud ephemerist Ute Margaret Flynn explains: "Flushed with excitement, perhaps a little drunk, Gruen promised a future dominated by Viennese shopping agoras, *PROUN*s he called them. He felt himself retracing the steps of Dr. Freud inside the Ringstrasse, 'into an American Prater, a shopper's Coney Island.'"

In 1986 the Hungarian computer designer Zsolt Bohus spotted the article. He became obsessed with developing it into a computer game for American providers outsourcing to Hungary. The Bohus game design, with steam and prairie fires and nightmare rides, with the superego spitting venom and the preconscious boiling and spewing, went out for review to test its commercial potential. It finally passed to Fred Blazs, an executive at an American game company (name withheld); also married to a psychiatrist (thus, he seemed the logical choice). However, Blazs explained that first of all, he had just been divorced; and secondly, in court his wife complained publicly that he had no unconscious at all. And on top of all that: what is the reward system for psychotherapy? "Remember these are kids passing puberty, in their underwear, playing computer games at two in the morning." Blazs was famous in the industry for saying: "In the next hundred years, we all will pass puberty over and over again, in game after game." That certainly would not qualify him as Freudian.

This Freud game (simply called *id*) does not get past the radar at Disney's Epcot Center either. Besides, why would Disney want visitors to discover their own unconscious? Indeed, Frida's warnings had come to roost. Mass culture was now shaping unconscious drives en masse, warp drives. It was building user-friendly wish fulfillment—ergonomically scripted spaces, what Klein calls consumer Calvinism: the myth of free will in a world of absolute predestination. We no longer can easily separate the latent from the manifest. As an editorial in a recent advertising journal explains, "Consumers don't need an unconscious, only better medication. An unexamined life shops."

As for Young Yussell—our only link to Frida and M+K—he winds up in America, first in Pittsburgh, brought there by his father, a pesky old man with a taste for bad advice and schnapps. When Yussell was twelve and still herding goats in Hungary, his father wrote, "Yussell, some day I will bring the entire family here to Pittsburgh. But you as the oldest son must get ready. Only one skill can save you in America. Learn this one thing, and you will be a success. Learn to play the violin."

So Yussell spent the next eight years sawing away at a cheap violin, then through his aunt, the rooming-house owner in Budapest, he got a slightly better tuned, perhaps stolen, violin, as a birthday present.

But imagine how useless playing the violin was when Yussell arrived in 1928. By the time he learned English, Pittsburgh was sinking into the Great Depression. Yussell eventually used his fine motor skills to become a kosher butcher.

His father, the boozy son of M+K, had other plans altogether. He decided to retire the moment that his sons arrived in Pittsburgh and refine his love of schnapps and other sweet whiskies (Southern Comfort, single-malt scotch whiskies, Glenfarclas when he could afford a pint). Finally, the family moved to Brooklyn, where he became a rag man, wheeling his little wagon behind movie theaters to watch an afternoon double bill. Then after ma'arev (evening prayer, with honey cake and schnapps), he would return home exhausted from the long day, itching for another pick me up.

Yussell married, though not happily. He fathered two children, who spent most of their formative years wishing they were somewhere else. Finally, Yussell brought them to Coney Island, as if following a voice from a dead relative—an insistent woman's voice that came to him in a haze and usually filled him with bad advice. But at least she just whispers, he reasoned. Taking advice from this voice, Yussell developed an unerring instinct for moving to neighborhoods just as they started to decline.

Coney Island began to sink like a stone almost the day after he arrived, or at least within the year.

His son, Norman (often confused with the author of this piece), was an anxious, fretful child, afraid of his own shadow, also afflicted, in Yussell's words, with "no common sense." What's more, Norman began to have strange nightmares after they moved to Coney Island, particularly about a woman with large glowing eyes like a mole. Luckily, Norman never remembers his dreams.

But something obviously lingered, like sour breath after a heavy meal. In 1995, while teaching media classes to computer animators, Norman became obsessed with Freud in Coney Island. As if by intuition, he began imagining a game he called Sim-Freud.

By 1998, this game settled in his mind like a pigeon on a ledge. One night, while he slept, a particle from a down pillow went into his ear. It imbalanced his canal. He woke up with benign positional vertigo. Suddenly, he couldn't distinguish front from back. The wind blowing on his face felt like a blast of air behind him. When he walked, the floor rose like liquid, rising and churning. But gradually, his brain made adjustments. It did not repair the imbalance, simply adjusted to it. His brain told his eyes to stop feeling nauseous or dizzy. That made upside-down appear right-side up. It adjusted his horizontal picture. Finally, he could walk easily.

But during the worst of the vertigo, when his head swam the most, Norman researched the history of dizzy spells. He learned about Prosper Ménière's Syndrome (1799–1862); and the French filmmaker who called himself La Ménière, because he suffered from severe vertigo for thirty years—from repetitive paroxysmal vertigo. But even stranger still, La Ménière spent his entire career in a serious pickle. As a young man, he managed to find a loyal backer named Labrouste, a gentle laconic commodities investor. Labrouste's blind trust led to a very unusual contract. He would pay La Ménière everything up front, entirely before shooting began. Then when the film was done, La Ménière could itemize his budget and return any unspent money.

For a few early shorts, that worked fine, but then Labrouste died unexpectedly, leaving no time to arrange his estate. So their unusual contract remained as part of the will. Legally La Ménière inherited a special fund but could lose all of it, every franc, the moment that he actually finished a film. He could drag out his preproduction work, rewrite for years, shoot and edit for a decade, even nearly complete as many films as he liked—and for each, draw another fifty thousand francs. But the moment any proof came to the heirs that he had actually finished a movie, they would set dogs of hell upon him.

So the legend grew about a secret cache of film cans, with movies about vertigo. Had La Ménière actually completed a dozen films? Was this five minutes by La Ménière the end of that two hours? Cults searched for secret premieres of his work, like alien sightings. Then clues to one of them caused a stir. Perhaps the reader has seen the recent article by Goldblatt on La Ménière's "unfinished" masterpiece: *Freud in New York*. As the movie opens, we see Freud struggling with vertigo, lying on the Persian rug on his famous couch. We enter his POV. Vertigo literally "uncoils" through traveling mattes. Strands of brain tissue rise in slender filaments, like floating gold leaf. Then Freud goes to the conference at Bremen and by boat to Manhattan. There, for more than an hour of the film, he is trapped in a sexual farce about phobias among New York socialites. One orgy leads to another, sexual penetrations pile up like vertigo inside an eloquent re-creation of a Manhattan hotel circa 1909. Finally the director, La Ménière himself, drops from the ceiling. We see him in his familiar rumpled tuxedo. He screams obscenities at the camera. The camera follows him picking up the last two minutes of the movie, a tail of celluloid a hundred feet long. Cackling like a rooster, he sets the last two minutes on fire. Soon the movie frame itself starts to burn. Flames literally engulf La Ménière. He escapes by slithering up the wall, almost like a lizard, and disappears.

Recently, the heirs have gone to court to argue that this is an ending. But for Freudian ephemerists, it may be a beginning. Folio 7 proves La Ménière correct. In the passage leading to the Coney Island episode, Freud writes that he and Fliess did indeed suffer occasionally from vertigo, from "dizzy nerves" caused by stress. Of course, can we trust what anyone, even great figures, write about their afflictions? Freud also added: "When vertigo took me over, grains of truth just slipped through my fingers."

In 2004, Norman introduced the Sim-Freud problem to the German filmmaker Eckhart Schmidt. That inspired Schmidt to begin a screenplay. He is still trying to get Al Pacino to play Freud. The story opens with a perverse angle of the Statue of Liberty. From there, an ocean liner zooms in on Freud, Jung, and Ferenczi at the bow, trading insults and insights, like Cole Porter songs about therapy. After the opening credits, we enter a swank 1909 libertine world, from Fifth Avenue to Harlem. Bits of business overlap. The master scene unfolds. Bawdy hostesses try to coax Dr. Freud into playing the rabbi at orgies, to deliver the hard truths about their afflicted lives. Reluctant to be a seer for these idiots, Freud struggles to find a moment by himself. He escapes with Jung to Coney Island. After gloomy but comic encounters, we follow him running like a tottering old man down the beach. He drops his cigar on an oil rag, and through a chain of sparks, accidentally sets fire to Dreamland.

It is like Orpheus in slapstick. Freud descends into a farcical underworld. Amazingly enough, production has indeed begun. An imaginary Coney Island has been built in Munich, mostly indoors. At Babelsberg, near Berlin, a faux Manhattan will double as Vienna—only a hundred meters from the famous Caligari Halle, where the German Expressionist film industry began in 1919 (now a skating rink). Throughout the orgy scenes, even one set on the ice, with music and Viennese ragtime dancing—as New York turns into a cross-dressing erogenous zone—Freud is plagued by an attack of vertigo; much the way Schmidt was struck by vertigo in 2002. What's more, various crew members claim that they hear voices from dead relatives. But a nervous grip (who refused to give his name) said that "movie sets are always infected with psychic rumors. It's as common as overdoses. Half the cast is usually possessed by something expensive and exhausting."

Indeed, the ninety years of coincidence that link Sim-Freud to seemingly everything must be seen as historical, not psychic. We cannot let Jungian or Rankian mysticism confuse us here. Years before Schmidt's movie was even imagined, back in 1999, Norman Klein introduced Sim-Freud to media artist and theorist Lev Manovich. While meeting for overpriced coffee at the Beverly Hills Hotel, they decided to translate the story into an ironic data pilgrimage. They would let Sim-Freud span the entire twentieth century. Odder still, they met precisely one month before the discovery of the Ephemera was announced at a conference in Rotterdam (where Edgar A. Poe pretended that Hans Pfall was first sighted, after a flight to the moon, in 1835). Over the course of a weekend, Klein and Manovich concocted a data narrative and called it *The Freud-Lissitzky Navigator.* Lev went to work designing it. Much of the text stayed in Lev's Russian-inflected English, like a ghostly filter.

Meanwhile, Norman heard the ghost of his great-grandfather M+K rising to complain. A rasping sound, vaguely like a human voice, ached in the back of his head, as if a synapse were pressing against a nerve. This was not the first time. Back in 1967, a hippie mystic in Montreal had warned Norman that his great-grandfather bore a grudge. The mystic spotted Norman doodling, then walked up to him.

"You have lived in two worlds and are lost in a third," he explained. Norman vaguely agreed.

Then he added: "Your great-grandfather danced in Europe. He is angry with you, perhaps unfairly, but you must do something." Norman was supposed to leave the doodle under a tree and pour a glass of water over it—that weekend or never at all—to soothe the old man's nagging spirit.

Of course Norman forgot to bother with all that, simply overslept, even lost the doodle altogether. Afterward, his emotional life was lost at sea for twenty-five years. Electronic equipment often crashed, even went on fire spontaneously, when he sat near it. His strange luck became a running joke. Finally, belatedly, late at night in 2004, he offered this novella to M+K. It was nearly three in the morning when he decided. He set his mind to conjuring a picture. He imagined an old man trying never to go back to that dreary farm. Legend has it that when M+K was ninety-seven years old, he would sit near the kitchen, waiting for women to pass by, then reach for a last squeeze of their hips, to restore his intimate memories before it was too late.

Feeling a trifle silly setting paper on fire, Norman listened for M+K's voice. A groan under the floor awakened. Something like a voice spoke in a very foreign language that Norman, never good at languages, still understood. It was a rare pleasure. The voice told him a secret about his father, of Young Yussell's first encounter with a prostitute provided by M+K in Hungary. Yussell's penis was so cold from waiting outside, he was embarrassed, needed help, and, for a moment, thought prostitutes knew how to make men happy, would be patient with him. M+K made Norman promise to never put this story in print. But Norman has clearly decided to break that promise.

Of course, that's Norman speaking, not me. I will maintain scholarly objectivity to the end, even the middle. And as long as my medication holds out, I am a man of Apollonian good spirits, not a neurotic who keeps confessing (but lying) to strangers, as Norman does. You undoubtedly have read about that unflattering incident in Canada, near the ancient forest. His passport has finally been restored, but it took some legal finagling.

I repeat, as I have said so often, it is nearly impossible in this culture not to erase your own identity. Think of what Freud's Ephemera has taught us, how little we knew before. Freud constantly erased exceptions to his theory in order to keep going. I am particularly fond of the five pages he called "The Psychopathology of the Stomach: Daydreams On How to Gut a Fish" (Folio 8, orange insert), with that Talmudic commentary on mushrooms (in tiny handwriting) and references to young women who eerily resembled his wife when she was young, but with one feature improved—a better neck, or tighter hips, the nose sharpened, the thighs leaner. Or Freud's line about the stomach as dreamwork, where he discusses transpathologies inside the body (again, mention they spoke to him). Freud even wondered if the autonomic nervous system cathects like the mind, if the stomach could be part of the id (*ich*).

Of course he scraps all this as nitwit chatter along with his recurring dreams that "smell" of Coney Island. Mass culture must be kept at a safe distance, a blind parallel to consciousness, like the stomach. So too with media. In Folio 5, he writes: "I just had a grueling phone conversation with Dora. The telephone mummifies me. It dries out my flesh but keeps the skin intact."

We return to 1909 in America, to make sense of this final clue: At last, a day after Coney Island, Freud got to see a wild porcupine. Abe Brill and Stanley Hall both made sure to find one. He was also mildly impressed by Niagara Falls (where the annoying comment, "Let the old gentleman go first" may have taken place).

Then accidentally Frida is told about about Sabina Spielrein (can Ferenczi ever keep his mouth shut? Or did Jung put his arms around Frida "poetically"?). With Sabina on her mind, she reads something very intimate to Freud on the telephone, something about therapy being a masturbatory pleasure similar to entertainments in Coney Island.

Here Freud's penmanship changes. In the margin, he doodles concentric "fleshlike" objects, perhaps sexualized telephone receivers (see Goldblatt again). We sense his infatuation with things that deliver "passionate withdrawal," eccentric distance. In 1910 (Folio 9), he calls the telephone "erogenous vapors."

While she chatters on, Freud agrees with Frida's "theories" once again; and it was not like him to agree that often with women in long-term therapy. He agrees that a Coney Island attraction—where a thousand people watch themselves stripped naked, metaphorically speaking—is like a machine inventing desire. Whoever controls that desire might be able to "colonize primal process." But this is not simply pornography, he insists. After a pause on the line, Frida agrees with Freud, saying, "Yes, pornography is not as passionate as the machines in Coney Island."

Freud holds the phone for a minute after Frida hangs up, as if the electricity inside the receiver were completing her message. Then he crosses something out in his notes so thoroughly that even laser searching cannot quite lift it.

That brings me to another problem, about laserographic confocal search methods. You'll excuse my drift, but perhaps you are following the legal campaign against laser searches (LCSM) in the U.S. and the European Union. What rights to privacy do the dead possess? I say none. (Norman worries too much. He probably thinks they need attorneys.) He retells that story about Young Yussell opening a side of beef at the store. Ghosts used to rattle between the floorboards, like rats mating. Eventually, customers spread the word about the ghosts. Business picked up, making Yussell unconsciously nervous. He was afraid if he hired someone, the man could be a thief. So Yussell made customers pay a little extra to hear what the ghosts were saying. Apparently ghosts cannot keep secrets. They love to gossip about the living. Very soon, every customer's bad habits turned into a public joke. In less than a month, business went back to normal (except the week of Halloween). "For the dead," Yussell explained, "human problems are the only pleasure they have left. It's what they do for a living, the same as cutting meat from dead animals."

At first, you enjoy the public shame. Your bad habits go on display. You and your close friends make fun of your naked truths. Replacing intimacy with embarrassment can be entertaining, like pornography. It becomes a simulation of therapy, an animatronic, behaviorist friend. In 1925 Freud writes about psychoanalysis being "watered down," like an entertainment. "Many abuses, mostly unrelated, find cover under its name. In America, too, psychoanalysis comes in conflict with Behaviorism, a theory which is naïve enough to boast that it has put the whole problem of psychology out of court."

It seems that Freud was the pot calling the kettle black. In the Ephemera, he lets us know what he was thinking while his patients

39

sound echoes in our shoes. We turn the echo into language: We sense that we have missed the train.

Evolution tends to favor animals that can sniff out these sounds, "scent" phonons. Humans are the exception. They tend to single-mindedly shut out this noise. As Freud discovered, we censor or filter these urgent traces of memory, particularly in our sleep. At the same time, humans are tantalized by these sounds, as if they were an erogenous zone, what some call "the siren effect." Clusters of molecular sounds excite our senses, even terrify us, but also seduce us. They are the puzzle left by a ghost. They speak, but generally in fragments, as in a dream. They rarely complete the sentence, the point of the words. Humans feel driven to complete the meaning instead; we are bred to do it, like a dog is bred to hunt or fill a hole. When a molecular "voice" forwards something that only molecules can decode, the human brain doesn't care. It will go to great lengths to complete it anyway—by instinct. Human beings have evolved a unique skill; they can imagine completeness, even when it is not there. That skill to misremember and misspeak has grown the size of our brains. It makes us intelligent enough to outwit animals with powerful jaws. In all the world, we may be the only species that can make fictions out of absences, that can pray to a molecule.

As with all new media, the theology surrounding nanoscopy will pass soon enough. Utopia lasts until the investors move in. Then it transforms into another violent business, another WMD. But nano-sounding—as it is called in the defense industry—may also overload us psychically in valuable new ways. (I don't share Norman's hope that phonon overload can protect us against ourselves. Apparently, when too much memory is repressed, the overload causes migraines and strokes. Norman thinks headaches, like avoidance therapy, can put an end to the history of forgetting.) But since Freud's day—symbolized by the nervous buzz that got to him in Coney Island—we have lived in variations of overload. They make us anxious, turn us violent, then and now. They are clusters of dynamic sound that we scent like a dog hearing an earthquake, like a Boccioni painting of the city vibrating (1910). This overload will now be industrially engineered. We will all become ghosts.

Over the next decade, we enter the age when phonons left by the dead may be harvested, going back to two hundred years, through nanoscopy. That is intentional overload. It is the next fretful step in the era launched by the discovery of Freud's Ephemera (1999). Very soon, we will ephemerize traces from a thousand people in the way that Freud did for himself. The bleeding through has begun. At the same time, the era preceding nanoscopy has ended. Its beginnings and its conclusion were earmarked by Freud and his Ephemera, by the screen that he used to keep his memories private. Now, in place of isolated Coney Island noise, a new feudalism is growing in the United States, as I said earlier, dominated by a globalized Coney Island, by machines that harvest and industrialize collective desire. It is an industrial form of "the invaded unconscious," something Freud absolutely refused to imagine, except perhaps on his deathbed, at the start of World War II. But now I repeat myself, like the sounds in a molecule, ever fainter each time. I am dreaming on my feet, caught in a crowd.

Above: Admission ticket for Steeplechase Park, ca. 1918.
pages 44–45: Sketch for funhouse mirrors by Albert Grass.
pages 46–47: Elevations of three pavilions for Dreamland: "The Dream Work Factory,"
"The Psychic Censor," and "The Libido," by Albert Grass.
pages 48–49: Model of Albert Grass's proposed Dreamland amusement park (restored 2009).

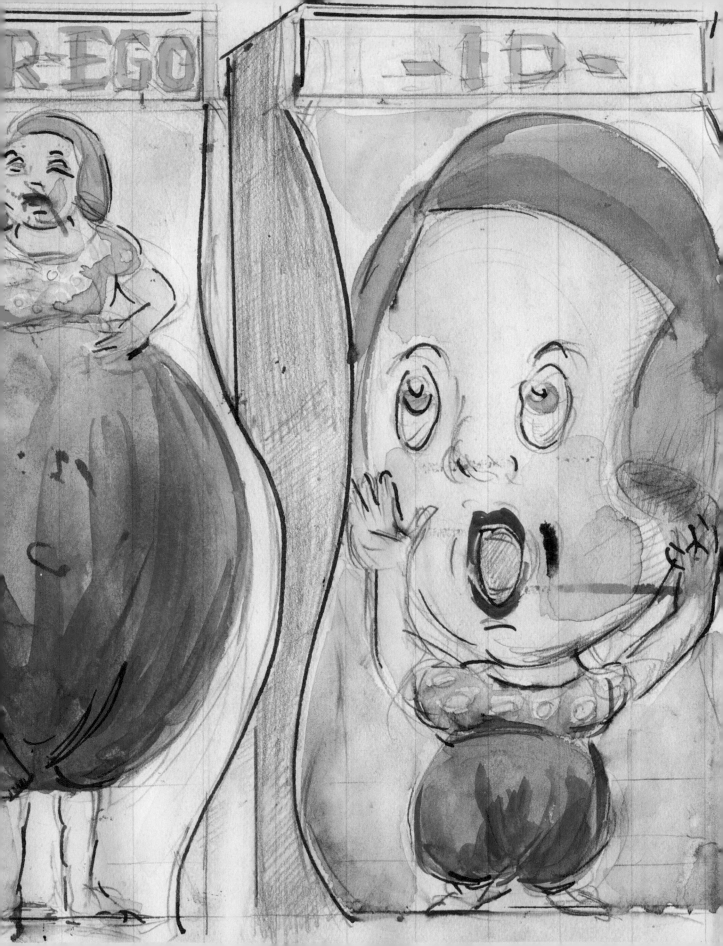

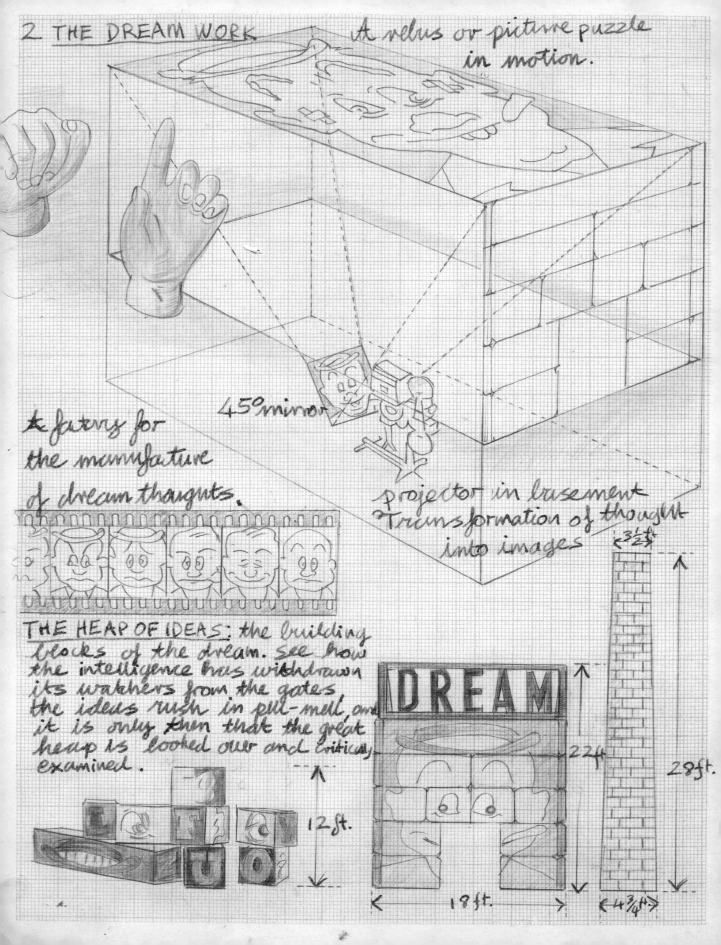

2. THE DREAM WORK

A rebus or picture puzzle in motion.

45° mirror

A factory for the manufacture of dream thoughts.

projector in basement
Transformation of thought into images

THE HEAP OF IDEAS: the building blocks of the dream. see how the intelligence has withdrawn its watchers from the gates, the ideas rush in pell-mell, and it is only then that the great heap is looked over and critically examined.

DREAM

12 ft.

22 ft.

3½ft.

28 ft.

18 ft.

4¾ ft.

3. THE PSYCHIC CENSOR

4. THE LIBIDO

The censor is the guardian of our psychic health. One among four dream-molders with which we are familiar. It builds a facade for the dream, a rational and intelligible exterior.

private

rear entrance

rotating platform

1 r.p.m. motor

CENSOR

43 ft.

29 ft.

20 ft.

Libido

50 ft.

26 ft.

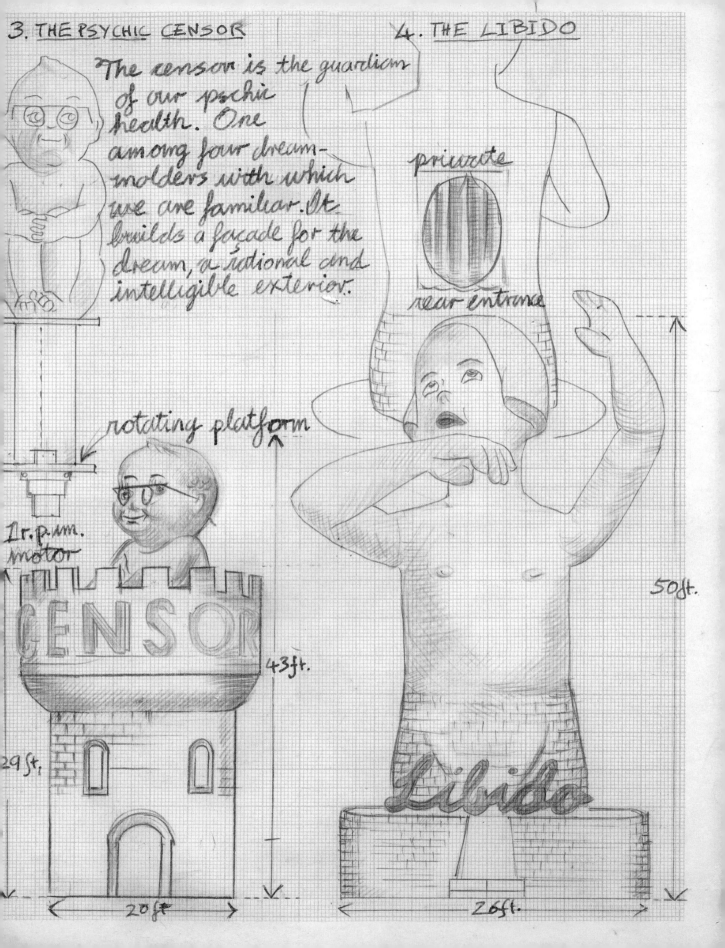

LITTLE BLUE BOOK NO. 1279
Edited by E. Haldeman-Julius

Side-Show Tricks Explained

Sword Swallowing, Fire Eating, Feats of Strength, Juggling Secrets, Etc.

Hereward Carrington

AN INTRODUCTION TO
THE CONEY ISLAND AMATEUR
PSYCHOANALYTIC SOCIETY

Zoe Beloff

"We are all freaks on the inside."
Albert Grass

A CHANCE ENCOUNTER

When Aaron Beebe, the director of the Coney Island Museum, invited
me to create an exhibition to celebrate the centennial of Sigmund Freud's
visit to Dreamland, there was no way I could say no. I have a long-standing
fascination with psychoanalysis and Coney Island, and this was a once
in a lifetime opportunity. I just had no idea how to proceed. Freud's own
notes on his visit, chronicled by Norman M. Klein in "Freud in Coney
Island," are in the collection of the Freud Museum in London. The idea of
simply presenting reproductions of his diary alongside photographs of the
attractions that he mentions such as "Hell Gate" and "Creation" seemed too
dry. I wanted to convey the deep relationships that exist between popular
imagination and the amusement park, to demonstrate how our unconscious
drives cathect with these fantastic structures. But how to show this?

In my work as an artist, I explore ways to manifest graphically the
unconscious processes of the mind and discover how they intersect with
technologies of the moving image. In the early 1990s I started collecting
home movies for my film *A Trip to the Land of Knowledge* (1994). I
wanted to find a way to reveal what Freud called "the psychopathology

Opposite: Side-Show Tricks Explained: Sword Swallowing, Fire Eating, Feats of
Strength, Juggling Secrets, Etc., *by Hereward Carrington. Carrington was a well-known
investigator of psychic phenomena. He wrote to solicit Freud's opinion on this subject in
1921. Freud replied that while he did not dismiss the study of parapsychology out of hand, he
wished to demarcate psychoanalysis clearly from this as yet unexplored sphere of knowledge.*

of everyday life," to show how these naïve family films, like dreams or slips of the tongue, reveal more than they ever intended about the darker unconscious dynamics of parents and children. In my interactive cinema CD-ROM *Beyond* (1997), I explored how writers and philosophers like Henri Bergson as well as psychologists Sigmund Freud and Pierre Janet conceptualized memory and the unconscious in relation to the birth of mechanical reproduction. I rephotographed old home movies and early films from the Library of Congress to create many short films, opening up an ambiguous space. Were the women whose images flickered on the screen really the hysterics documented in particular case histories described in the narration? This unresolved state between sound and image opened up a void, a space to wonder what the moving image can reveal…a space between seeing, imagining, and projecting.

My starting point is always historical records and documents. But I want to find ways to document the intangible, images that "are not there." I have created stereoscopic séances based on accounts of spirit mediums. I have attempted to show the world through the eyes of patients suffering from mental disturbance, to transmit experience of hallucinations and delirium. I have explored psychoanalysts' own attempts to document their patients on film in the 1920s and 30s.[1] I think of myself as being a medium, an interface between the living and the dead, the real and the virtual world of images and sounds. As an artist my role is, I think, simply to be spoken through…an antenna attuned to vibrations moving across time. So how could I tune myself to the denizens of Coney Island's vivid history?

I kept coming back to one particular film in my collection titled *The Lonely Chicken Dream* by a woman named Beverly d'Angelo. I acquired it in the early 1990s at the flea market on Sixth Avenue in Manhattan. Beverly's husband, Buster, had been a keen amateur filmmaker. The story of the family's postwar rise in prosperity unspools through his home movies as the family moves from a tenement in Brooklyn to suburban New Hyde Park in Long Island.

Among all the rolls of 16mm film, *The Lonely Chicken Dream* stood out. It was the only film by Buster's wife, and it purported to depict a dream and then interpret it. In the film, Beverly dreams that she returns for an afternoon of fun at Coney Island, where she grew up. She goes on one wild ride after another. On awakening, she confronts the grim reality that her husband is having an affair with her best friend, Betty, and that it is her marriage that is a rollercoaster ride. The idea of a housewife

Stills from The Lonely Chicken Dream *by Beverly d'Angelo. A Brooklyn housewife articulates her frustration with her philandering husband, Buster.*

reenacting her dream on film to articulate her dissatisfaction with her marriage in the 1950s before Betty Friedan and women's liberation seemed all too strange. Could this Brooklyn housewife have known about Freud and his *Interpretation of Dreams?* The idea seemed ridiculously farfetched. The film languished in my collection simply because I couldn't believe it.

Wondering how to proceed with the exhibition, I found myself imagining possibilities for this film. What if it were just the tip of the iceberg, a single piece of a larger archive? I began to speculate. Perhaps she was part of an amateur cine club in which everyone explored their dreams, something like the Amateur Cine League of dreams right here in Brooklyn. It seemed too fantastic, yet I couldn't shake the idea.

I think of the flea market as a beach where people's earthly possessions wash up after they pass on. Sometimes, if I concentrate hard enough, I've discovered there are times when I can find something I really want amidst the great random tide of discarded objects swirling around me. I've had

some uncanny moments where I turned around and found something very unusual and unique, the exact object I pictured in my mind's eye. I'd find myself trembling, unsure that what I was looking at was entirely real.

I walked into the garage on Twenty Sixth Street, all that is left of the once sprawling lots. Much to my surprise, Paul, the vendor who sold me the d'Angelo film, was still there. He recognized me and asked if I was still looking for home movies. I said, "Yes, but right now I am working on a project about Coney Island. Do you have anything?" Paul lives in Coney Island and told me he would ask around. "Come back next week," he said.

One week later I unpacked three large cardboard boxes of what appeared to be home movies, snapshots, notes, and knickknacks from the estate sale of one Robert Troutman. My hands were shaking. I was on the floor surrounded by old newspaper, rusty cans that smelled of vinegar, torn photo albums, crumbling letters. I was ecstatic. This was none other than the archive of the Coney Island Amateur Psychoanalytic Society. I thought of Walter Benjamin's words as he unpacked his library: "Every passion borders on the chaotic, but the collector's passion borders on the chaos of memories."[2] I soon realized that Beverly d'Angelo was indeed a member of this Society and *The Lonely Chicken Dream* belongs with the collection. How much more material, films, lecture notes, correspondence, still exists in attics and basements? One can only speculate. What you see here at the museum is, I hope, just the beginning.

Fortunately I was able to track down Robert Troutman, who recently relocated from New York to a retirement community outside Miami. He was kind enough to share his reminiscences of this very unique society, to my knowledge the only amateur psychoanalytic society that has existed in this country. Robert, who used the name "Bobby Beaujolais," was one of the last members. When the Society folded in the early 1970s, he had the forethought to pack up the archive, which remained in his basement until his move to Florida.

The Coney Island Amateur Psychoanalytic Society did not spring directly from Freud's visit to the amusement park in the summer of 1909. It was inaugurated in 1926 by Albert Grass, the visionary amusement park designer. From what I was able to piece together from public records

Opposite: The office of the Coney Island Amateur Psychoanalytic Society above the Shore Theater, 1301 Surf Avenue, Coney Island, 1940. Photograph taken for the purpose of real estate appraisal for taxation.

and notes he kept on file at the Society's office, it appears that Grass first encountered Freud's writing on his tour of duty in France in the Signal Corps during the First World War.

I have to confess, for me, Grass is truly a kindred spirit, an artist, a technologist, and a dreamer. I love to pore over old manuals; in fact I already had copies of Audel's *New Electric Library* and was delighted to find his well-thumbed editions filled with notes that spiraled into flights of fancy, where I glimpsed his first attempts to construct a three-dimensional map of the mind. I had created an installation inspired in part by this series of books, *The Influencing Machine of Miss Natalija A.* It included a stereoscopic diagram or phantogram of an imaginary machine as described by the schizophrenic patient of one of Freud's early followers, Victor Tausk, a machine that she believed influenced her mind and body. But I had never imagined something as ambitious as Grass's visionary plans for a great amusement park that would embody the workings of the unconscious as put forth by Freud in chapter seven of *The Interpretation of Dreams.*

THE EYE OF CONSCIOUSNESS

Legend has it that before the Great War Albert Grass got his start as a boy working in the notorious "Insanitarium with Blowhole Theater" for George Tilyou, the owner of Steeplechase Park, Coney Island's great Pavilion of Fun.[3] After the armistice in 1918, he was hired by Edward, George Tilyou's son, to design new attractions.

Grass returned to Coney Island with a vision that would become a lifelong quest, to rebuild the Dreamland amusement park that he loved as a child as a true "Dreamland," constructed according to strict Freudian principles. Sadly, his vision never materialized. Funding was not forthcoming. What remains are only his sketches, plans, and a working model commissioned by William Mangels's Coney Island Museum of American Recreation. One can conceptualize his design as a missing link between the Beaux Arts structures of the original Dreamland that burned down in 1911 and the high modernism of the 1939 World's Fair.

For example, Grass's plan for the pavilion representing "consciousness," a great glowing, revolving head with two staring eyes, seems to look back to designs for the Globe Tower that was proposed for Coney

Opposite: Elevation of the "Consciousness" pavilion by Albert Grass, 1930.

4. CONSCIOUSNESS
A beacon of light

THE DREAM IMPULSE
THE BEGINNINGS
OF THE DREAM,
IT'S MOTIVE
POWER, ORIGINATES
IN THE UNCONSCIOUS.
IT STRIVES TO GAIN
ADMISSION TO
CONSCIOUSNESS.
DURING THE DAY
THERE IS A CONTINU-
OUS COURSING STREAM
FROM THE PSI SYSTEM
OF PERCEPTION
(EYEBALL) TOWARDS
MOTILITY. THIS CEASES AT
NIGHT AND NO LONGER HINDERS
A STREAM OF CURRENT
EXCITEMENT IN
THE OTHER
DIRECTION.

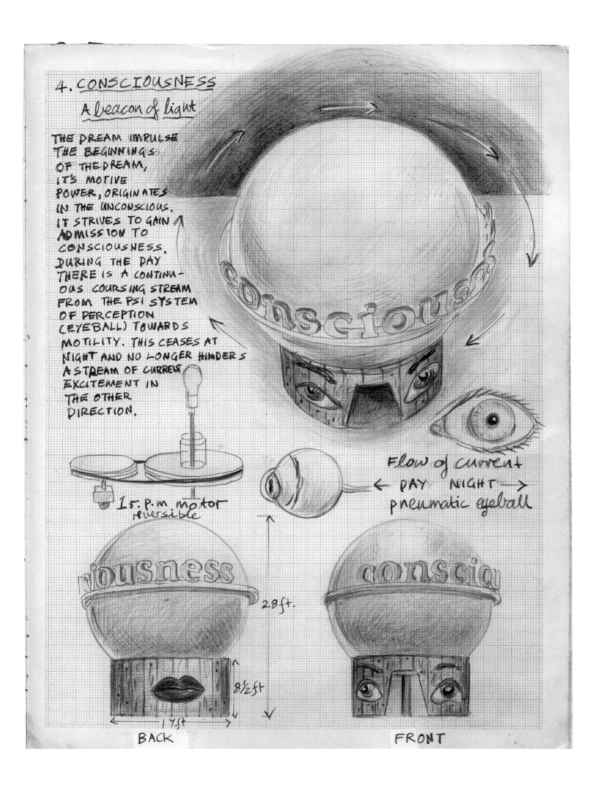

1 r.p.m. motor
reversible

Flow of current
← DAY   NIGHT →
pneumatic eyeball

28ft.

8½ft

17ft

BACK

FRONT

Left: Postcard, the Steel Globe Tower, 700 feet high, Coney Island, N.Y., ca. 1905.
Right: Postcard, the Trylon and the Perisphere, New York World's Fair, 1939.

Island in 1906, while prefiguring the famous Perisphere of the World of Tomorrow a decade later.[4] But more fascinating still, this head also looks forward to the original "Surrealist House" designed by Julian Levy and Ian Woodner for the Amusement Zone adjacent to the World's Fair.

Levy and Woodner's prospectus showed a house built in the shape of an eye with a fantastically convoluted interior. "It proposed to construct a surrealist walk through…in the manner of the old type 'funny house' but with each attraction turned into terms of surrealism, based accurately on surrealist theory and principles—thus the 'funny house' of tomorrow." Their proposal went on to explain in "oversimplified terms," that it was "an attempt to utilize scientifically the mechanisms of inspiration and imagination…and apply this research to a systematic reformation of reality."[5] Of course the surrealists were fascinated by Freud's theories. The eye was the symbol of surrealism, but one wonders whether the idea of building a fairground funny house to celebrate the unconscious could have perhaps originated in Grass's head. Were cosmopolitan, Harvard-educated New Yorkers Levy and Woodner aware of Albert Grass's designs and the activities of the Coney Island Amateur Psychoanalytic

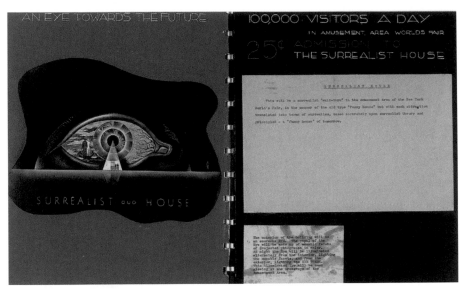

Julian Levy and Ian Woodner, "Surrealist House," 1938. This is the original proposal for a surrealist concession at the 1939 World's Fair. The commission ultimately went to Savador Dalí, who scandalized fairgoers with his "Dream of Venus" pavilion.

Society? This is just one of many tantalizing questions raised by the discovery of their archive.

Similarly, parallels can be drawn between Grass's design for his central figure the "Libido," the giant topless goddess "Creation" guarding the entrance of the original Dreamland and Dalí's "Dream of Venus," which was the ultimately realized version of "Surrealist House" at the World's Fair. At the beginning of the century visitors entered the amusement park under the outstretched wings of "Creation." In 1939 they entered the "Dream of Venus" pavilion between the skinny plaster spread legs, gartered stockings, and frilly slip of an unseen giantess. While Grass's "Libido" pavilion was not as racy as Dalí's, his sketches show how visitors would enter a fifty-foot building in the shape of a prepubescent girl, through a doorway at the level of her crotch.

The other clue to Grass's connection with the more scholarly world of psychoanalysis was a book that I found in the archives: *Side-Show Tricks Explained: Sword Swallowing, Fire Eating, Feats of Strength, Juggling Secrets, Etc.*, by Hereward Carrington, inscribed "to my dear friend and seeker after truth, Albert Grass." Carrington was a British investigator of

*The Coney Island Amateur Psychoanalytic Society's annual "Dream Film" award
dinner, 1949.*

psychic phenomena who had moved to the United States, where he worked
with the American Society for Psychical Research. He corresponded with
Freud on the subject of the paranormal. Although Carrington embraced
Freud's interpretation of dreams, the great psychoanalyst was somewhat
skeptical of occult phenomena. To help him in his task of unmasking
fraudulent mediums, Carrington went to Coney Island to study the tricks
of sideshow artists. It was on one of those expeditions that he met Grass,
who introduced him to many of his friends in the amusement business.
Grass was doubtless most impressed by a man who corresponded with
Freud himself, and he invited him to address the Society on the subject of
"Freudian Psychology and Psychical Research."[6]

In general, however, it appears that the members of the Coney Island
Amateur Psychoanalytic Society were self-taught Freudians poring over
dog-eared copies of *The Interpretation of Dreams* and *The Psychopathology
of Everyday Life*. Most of them were working-class men and women who

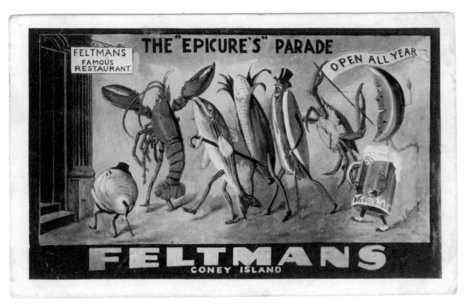

Postcard, April 1932. Charles Feltman invented the hot dog in 1870. His restaurant, Feltmans, was the largest in Coney Island, with an opulent range of dining rooms and beer gardens. The Society enjoyed meeting there through the 1930s.

couldn't afford to become professional psychoanalysts yet wanted to take part in the great intellectual adventures of the city. Like Freud, many were Jews. Some had studied psychology in college. This included, on one end of the social spectrum, Charmion de Forde, the society's only heiress, who went to Clark University, and on the other, Molly Lippman, who took night classes at City College while earning a living as a secretary in the garment district. Like many early converts, they believed that psychoanalysis could change the world, and they were braving moral outrage from a society who equated it with free love. One can think of them as working-class utopians, a link between the Workers Film and Photo League of the 1930s and today's YouTube activists and dreamers.

THE DREAM FILMS

According to minutes and letters, the Society met once a month for discussions, screenings, and lectures in a small office above the Shore Theater at 1301 Surf Avenue in Coney Island. Once a year they had a special celebration at Feltmans Restaurant, where the "dream films" were screened and a best-film winner chosen.

In 1926, soon after the Society was founded, Albert Grass proposed that members attempt to re-create their dreams on film and analyze them. He had worked as a cameraman in the Signal Corps during World War I and returned to Brooklyn with technical expertise.[7] When Kodak produced the first 16mm camera and the new "safety film" in 1923, the medium was born for the amateur. Grass was ready to initiate members of the Society into the mysteries of cinematography and Freudian theory. He firmly believed that the films would prove Freud's dictum that dreams are always the disguised fulfillment of a suppressed wish.

Of course not all members of the Society made dream films, but a surprising number did. Many of them, including Albert Grass and Arthur Rosenzweig, were also members of the Amateur Cine League. By an astonishing coincidence this organization was founded the very same year as the Society, 1926, in Brooklyn by a fifty-seven-year-old MIT graduate, Hiram Percy Maxim. Like Grass, Maxim had sweeping objectives, and like Grass he saw home movies as opening up a new form of knowledge. The scope of his thinking can be grasped from his first editorial: "Amateur cinematography has a future that the most imaginative of us would be totally incapable of estimating. When we analyze amateur cinematography we find it a very much broader affair than it appears upon the surface. Instead of its being a form of light individual amusement, it is really an entirely new method of communication. Our civilization offers us today only the spoken word or the written word as a means of communicating with each other. This word may be spoken to those within sound of our voice, telephoned over a hired wire, mailed in a letter or telegraphed in dots and dashes. But no matter how transmitted it is still the spoken or written word. We are dumb as far as movement, action, grace, beauty, and all that depends on these things. The motion picture communicates all of these. We are able to transmit what our eyes see, and it is the next thing to actually being present ourselves. And so instead of amateur cinematography being merely a means of individual amusement, we have in it a means of communicating a new form of knowledge to our fellow beings, be where they may upon the earth's surface."[8]

The League encouraged the formation of local clubs, offering advice on rules, contests, etc., and published such news of the clubs' activities as was submitted. It also invited ACL members to send in their own films for review. In December 1930 the fourth anniversary volume of *Amateur Movie Makers Magazine* announced a new feature: the annual selection

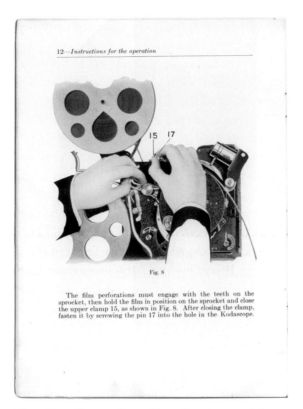

Fig. 8

The film perforations must engage with the teeth on the sprocket, then hold the film in position on the sprocket and close the upper clamp 15, as shown in Fig. 8. After closing the clamp, fasten it by screwing the pin 17 into the hole in the Kodascope.

Threading diagram from Albert Grass's copy of the projector manual "Instructions for Operating the Model B Kodascope."

of the ten best amateur films of the year. As a member of the League, Grass must have known Maxim and exchanged ideas. Perhaps it was the Amateur Psychoanalytic Society's own dream film competition that inspired Percy to follow suit with his ten-best list? But while the Amateur Cine League went on to be an international organization with thousands of members, the Coney Island Amateur Psychoanalytic Society does not appear to have attracted members beyond New York's five boroughs. Whether it began independently or was formed by Grass initially as a local branch of the ACL is hard to say, but it quickly became clear that his goals were far more radical. "Sigmund Freud has written that the royal road to the unconscious lies in our dreams. Each night we are plunged into a fantastical world as amazing as anything we see in Saturday night Photoplays. But how to capture the most effervescent of experiences so that they can be properly analyzed and recorded for future generations? The answer, my friends, lies in our new tools, the Cine-Kodak Camera and the Kodascope Projector, enabling us to reenact our dreams on film, producing a perfect reproduction of our mind's nocturnal wanderings, the strange adventures of our souls. As it will surely soon be with sound and color to perfect the illusion, we will open up our darkest dreams to the bright light of reason."[9]

Even in this brief quote, it is clear that Albert Grass is making a great conceptual leap beyond Maxim. While Maxim extols the ability of film to capture and share what we experience in our waking life, Grass grasps the oneiric potential of cinema. Where did this idea come from? After all, Freud himself inaugurated a great turning away from the visual to the verbal in the "talking cure." He refused to look at his patients on the couch. He believed that language, free association, slips of the tongue held the clues to our unconscious, the secrets that we keep buried even from ourselves.

My hypothesis is that Grass drew his inspiration from a rather literal reading of Freud's classic 1913 text, *The Interpretation of Dreams*. Here Freud discusses how wish fulfillment, that is the raison d'être of every dream, is often hard to discern because it is disguised, hidden from our inner moral censors by various procedures including the condensation and displacement of ideas and the dramatization of thoughts and desires in the form of "mental pictures." Thus, when we dream we do not experience a wish as an abstract, intangible concept; instead we find ourselves protagonists in a fully formed virtual world complete with characters we may or may not recognize from our waking life, caught up in strange and often suspenseful situations. One could argue, like Grass, that the closest waking analogy is narrative cinema.

Freud expresses what he called "regard for dramatic fitness" in dreams very clearly in these passages from *The Interpretation of Dreams*: "a thought, usually the one wished for, is in the dream made objective and represented as a scene or according to our belief as experience…On closer examination, it is plainly seen that there are two pronounced characters in the manifestations of the dream which are almost independent of each other. The one is the representation as a present situation with the omission of the 'perhaps,' the other is the transformation of the thought into visual pictures and into speech."[10] He discusses how "secondary elaboration" works like a good screenplay, to make the dream appear seamless and coherent, even suspenseful, to the

Frames from Coney Island, *1917. Albert Grass believed that its star and director Roscoe "Fatty" Arbuckle personified Freud's concept of the id.*

dreamer while in fact it is a conglomeration of many ideas that must be approached separately in the course of analysis.

If a dream is like a film in which the dreamer is the protagonist, why shouldn't the most fitting medium for sharing and analyzing a dream be cinema, now in the hands of ordinary people? In dreams the fantastic can occur: we can be in one place and then magically in another. Thus with a simple editing bench and a hot splicer even the amateur could create a fantastic celluloid dream world and then take it apart shot by shot in the course of analyzing and revealing the particular wish lurking within it.

A MONSTROUS ID

Freud's writing inspired Grass to initiate the dream film series that would become, for forty years, a tradition in the Society. At the same time it should be noted that Grass's own favorite movie was *Coney Island* (1917), directed by Roscoe "Fatty" Arbuckle, starring the fat man himself along with a young Buster Keaton.[11] As his notes indicate, Grass loved to entertain members with a screening followed by a lecture in which he showed how the movie articulated Freud's theory of the ego. Here Arbuckle is the embodiment of the most monstrous, charming, androgynous, and playful "id," freed from the rules of the civilized "ego" or the "superego" cops, even unbound from the confines of gender, regressing to a pure polymorphous, infantile state of unbound desire. Arbuckle was also the model for the obese clown in the animation that Grass planned to project onto the roof of the "Unconscious" pavilion in his proposed Dreamland.

That Grass articulated this long before film theorists took up psychoanalysis and before silent comedy was considered worthy of critical attention is extraordinary. Indeed, the one person in the 1920s who truly understood and expressed silent comedy's radical potential was Luis Buñuel in his essay *Buster Keaton's College* (1927).[12] Once again, this raises the question whether Grass was aware of the surrealists or whether they knew about him. At first the very idea seems absurd. Grass and his friends were working-class New Yorkers who did not see themselves as artists, let alone members of the avant-garde. They were simply trying to understand their own psyches because they believed that psychoanalysis promised a path to human happiness to which everyone is entitled. And yet tantalizing questions remain. During his stint in the Signal Corps in France in World War I, Grass was billeted near Nantes, where André Breton worked as an intern at the local hospital. Did the two of them ever meet? Did someone introduce him to Julian Levy, the art dealer and surrealist champion in New York?[13] And could that someone have been Charmion de Forde?

Charmion was the only member of the Coney Island Amateur Psychoanalytic Society who was wealthy and sophisticated. Her father was a Wall Street financier, and she briefly studied at Clark University. Her only surviving film, *The Praying Mantis* (1931), provides a single tantalizing clue that she was indeed familiar with the surrealist inner circle: an inter-title reads, "Mr. K. shrieks, 'You've been two timing me with Rrose. You little tramp." Was "Rrose" just a simple typo or a sly reference to Rrose Sélavy, Marcel Duchamp's female alter ego who emerged in 1921 in a series of photographs by Man Ray?

THE HISTORY OF DREAMS

This archive is a remarkable record of the hopes, fears, and fantasies of ordinary New Yorkers, a changing cross section of those who made up the fabric of Coney Island through the twentieth century, from immigrant Jews and Italians to wealthy bohemians to young gay men exploring their

Left: Rrose Sélavy. *Photograph by Man Ray of Marcel Duchamp, 1921.*
Right: Frames from Charmion de Forde's film, The Praying Mantis.

sexuality in the 1960s. Thinking about this project, I often come back
to a provocative statement by Walter Benjamin in his 1927 essay, *Dream
Kitsch*: "The history of the dream remains to be written, and opening
up a perspective on this subject would mean decisively overcoming the
superstitious belief in natural necessity by means of historical illumination."[14]

Benjamin says that while Freud was exploring the psychic make up of
the individual through the study of dreams, he was not thinking about
larger patterns of society and how a changing society influences our
unconscious. Benjamin imagined that a history of dreams might tell us
who we are in a social context rather than relegating the imagination to
a timeless, ahistorical sphere. It seems to me that this might indeed be a
perfect lens through which to view the Society's "dream films."

If the "dream films" seem poorly shot and at times little more than
clichéd home movies, one might agree with Benjamin that the era of
heroic or visionary dreams is over: "The dream has grown grey. The
grey coating of dust on things is its best part. Dreams are now a shortcut
to banality. Technology consigned the outer image of things to a long

farewell, like banknotes that are bound to lose their value." But Benjamin went on to write that it is through dreamwork that the banal, the kitsch, the outworn phrase is recuperated, because in the dream we understand the good that resides in these things.

Benjamin was perhaps the first cultural theorist to celebrate the ephemeral; he showed us that it is not through the big events but through the scraps and remains of everyday life that we can best understand history. I believe that through the intimate, private Coney Island "imaginary" represented by this archive we can get a unique glimpse of hopes, dreams, and anxieties of several generations of New Yorkers.

At the end of *Lay Analysis*, Freud wrote, "perhaps once more an American may hit on the idea of spending a little money to get the 'social workers' of his country trained analytically and to turn them into a band of helpers for combating a neurosis of civilization…aha! A new kind of salvation army! Why not?"[15] Freud's idea did not materialize. Psychoanalysis remained an expensive pastime of the upper classes. But the members of the Coney Island Psychoanalytic Society came closer than many to materializing his vision. They took difficult abstract European concepts and with a hands-on American spirit applied them to their own lives. In their own way they were visionaries who, undeterred by lack of finances or professional training, decided to explore their inner life, to share their dreams with each other and in doing so attempted to free the psyche from the constraints of class and of cultural and sexual mores of their time.

I am indebted to all who took the time to contribute their memories, most especially Robert Troutman, but also I'd like to mention Patricia White, who gave us permission to reproduce photographs of her great aunt Charmion de Forde; Gerald d'Angelo; and Bob Rosenzweig, who shared memories and snapshots of his favorite absentminded professor, Uncle Arthur.

Notes

1. Zoe Beloff, "Mental Images: The Dramatization of Psychological Disturbance," in Karen Beckman and Jean Ma, editors, *Still Moving: Between Cinema and Photography* (Durham, NC: Duke University Press, 2008), 226–52.

2. Walter Benjamin, "Unpacking My Library," in *Walter Benjamin: Selected Writings, Volume 2, 1927–1934* (Cambridge, Mass.: Belknap Press of Harvard University Press, 1999), 486.

3. In his essay "Freud in Coney Island" Norman Klein describes Freud's reaction to this descent into the id, where men and women were separated by demented clowns and women had their skirts blown up by jets of hot air to the amusement of the audience.

4. The proposed globe was planned to be the largest steel structure ever erected, 300 feet in diameter and 700 feet tall. It was to include a vaudeville theater, skating rink, four-ring circus, hotel, weather observatory, rollercoaster, and several dining establishments. Bonds were sold in 1906 and 1907; there were not one but two groundbreaking ceremonies. However, it never made it above the foundations. In 1908 the company's treasurer was arrested for absconding with stock proceeds. See Chad Randl, *Revolving Architecture: A History of Buildings That Rotate, Swivel, and Pivot* (New York: Princeton Architectural Press, 2008), 88.

5. Ingrid Schaffner, *Salvador Dalí's Dream of Venus: The Surrealist Funhouse from the 1939 World's Fair* (New York: Princeton Architectural Press, 2002), 38. Levy and Woodner's original plans did not come to fruition. Instead they hired the great artist, showman Salvador Dalí, who built the Dream of Venus pavilion.

6. This was a subject that Carrington fixated on for many years. See Hereward Carrington, "Freudian Psychology and Psychical Research (A Rejoinder)," *The Journal of Abnormal Psychology* 9 (6) (February 1915): 411–16.

7. It is difficult to know exactly what films Grass actually shot while in the Signal Corps. His notes mention *Plastic Reconstruction of a Face, Red Cross Worker, Paris 1918*. It is a strange, almost surreal film in which doctors, dressed in artist's smocks, are in a studio constructing false noses and ears for soldiers who had their faces destroyed by shrapnel in the war. The film is in the collection of the National Library of Medicine in Bethesda, Maryland.

8. For more information on the Amateur Cine League as well as lists of winning films from 1930 to 1994, see Alan D. Kattelle, "The Amateur Cinema League and Its Films," *Film History* 15 (2003): 238–51.

9. From Albert Grass, unpublished notes for his inaugural address at Feltmans Restaurant, Coney Island, July 25, 1926.

10. Sigmund Freud, *The Interpretation of Dreams*, trans. A. A. Brill (New York: Barnes and Noble, 2005), 422.

11. Grass would have access to this film through the *Kodascope Libraries*. Started in 1924 by William Beach Cook, Kodak began operating the *Kodascope Libraries* in the spring of 1925, around the United States in regional offices and local camera stores. An early precursor to the videotape rental store, Kodak leased negatives of fine-grain prints from a variety of Hollywood producers and made stunning amber- and sepia-tinted prints for rental. Most were comedies and newsreels. Grass would have been able to order both the Fleischer's Out Inkwell series and Comique/Paramount shorts of Roscoe Arbuckle.

12. Paul Hammond, *The Shadow and Its Shadow* (San Francisco: City Lights Books, 2000), 61.

13. Levy welcomed local surrealist talent. He exhibited the work of Joseph Cornell, the shy Christian Scientist who lived with his mother on Utopia Parkway in Flushing, Queens. Like Grass, Cornell made films using the amateur 16mm format.

14. Walter Benjamin, "Dream Kitsch: Gloss on Surrealism," in *Walter Benjamin: Selected Writings, Volume 2, 1927–1934* (Cambridge, Mass.: Belknap Press of Harvard University Press, 1999), 3.

15. Sigmund Freud, *The Question of Lay Analysis: Conversations with an Impartial Person*, trans. James Strachey (New York: W. W. Norton, 1978), 8.

pages 70–75: Dreamland sketches from the notebooks of Albert Grass, 1928.

the bright
light of reason
conscious

a clouded
consciousness

the ego
a facade that
conceals the id

A
DREA

the burgeoning of desire

The fat "lady"

the great da
of the unconsci
breast

the window of the

monstrous metamorphasising down

the brain

projector

45° mirror

The crazy house ⇒ The dream facto[ry]

hieroglyphs: translated
one by one into the
dream thoughts

IDEAS GO UP IN SMOKE

rubber

the interpretation of
dreams.

the key

DREAM WORK

THE DREAMER

THE MIDGET CRANE

Year: 1926
Filmmaker: Albert Grass
Transfer note: copied at 18 frames per second
from a 16mm black-and-white Kodak safety film original
Running time: 2 minutes 17 seconds

Albert Grass was the founder and first president of the Coney Island
Amateur Psychoanalytic Society. How he discovered Freud's writing
remains unclear, but it may have been during his service in the Signal
Corps during the First World War when he was stationed in France.
His experience as a military cameraman led to a fascination with the
expressive power of cinema. He inaugurated the Society's annual film
competition in which members submitted films that illustrated and
analyzed one of their dreams.

The Midget Crane is Grass's entry for the 1926 competition. The
film shows that Grass understood the ideas set forth by Freud in *The
Interpretation of Dreams.* The content of a dream is the fulfillment of
a wish. Dreams dramatize ideas in the process of which words are
transformed into moving images. Dreams refer to very recent and
unimportant events and to very important early childhood experiences. In
dreams, condensation fuses several ideas into one. And most important,
the manifest content of dreams hides their latent meaning.

In the opening titles, Grass states his particular dream wish: "to
tower over one's employer." His dream draws on his experience the day
before, when his boss, Edward Tilyou, made an anti-Semitic slur, calling
Grass an "ugly Jew." Grass shows us how in his dream he unconsciously
retaliated by turning these words into their Yiddish equivalent, *mies
Yid,* conjuring up a visual equivalent to the sound of these words, thus
shrinking Tilyou and his entire staff to the size of "midgets." The fact
that he imagined himself towering over them in a crane evokes both his
own sexual prowess, a crane being a phallic symbol, and refers to his job
as a designer of rides in Steeplechase Park that would have been erected
with a crane.

In the second part of the dream, Grass confines his boss to be burned
to death in "Lilliputia." This was a real place, a miniature reproduction
of fifteen-century Nuremberg populated by three hundred midgets,
one of Dreamland's most popular entertainments. Like the rest of the

Albert Grass (left) in the Signal Corps during the Meuse-Argonne offensive, 1918.

amusement park, it burned to the ground in 1911. This image may indeed be the key to Grass's own psychic trauma. We know that he witnessed the fire as a young boy, looking on helplessly as his father rushed in to save fellow employees from the terrible conflagration. This vision of hell may have been reinforced by Grass's more recent experiences in the trenches. In his dream he exorcises his own terror by punishing Tilyou.

Grass was too young to have filmed the fire himself. The footage he uses is not the destruction of the Lilliputian Village. It is a short clip from *Fighting the Flames, Dreamland* produced by the American Mutoscope and Biograph company in 1904, now in the Library of Congress Paper Print collection. This extraordinarily popular spectacle simulated a fire at a six-story hotel and featured a cast of 120 firefighters who had to rescue guests leaping from windows.

Grass's lifelong dream was to create a new Dreamland amusement park constructed in a fashion that would illustrate Freud's theory of dream formation. He produced sketches and plans but lacked the necessary capital. Over and over again he lobbied Tilyou to invest in his vision but without success. Edward Tilyou was the oldest son of George

C. Tilyou, who founded Steeplechase Park in 1908. By all accounts he was indeed an anti-Semite, unsurprising in an era when Jews were frequently victims of discrimination.

The last inter-title of the film, "I resolve to erect 'The Royal Road to the Unconscious' on the site of 'Sodom by the Sea,'" brings together two references that would have been familiar to his fellow members of the Society. Freud famously referred to dreams as "the royal road to the unconscious." "Sodom-by-the-sea" was an expression first used to refer to Coney Island in the 1870s but one that remained very much in the lingo. But by the time young Albert was growing up, the worst was over; as noted in a *New York Times* article on May 6, 1894, "The City of Brooklyn spread the blue coat of its police authority over Coney Island to-day, and for the first time in its history John Y. McKane's Sodom-by-the-sea became a respectable Sunday resort. The wooden elephant looked down on the wonderful transformation in utter astonishment and dismay." This was a rather optimistic assessment. Coney Island never lost its racy character, and the sexual innuendo of the expression would not have been lost on Albert Grass.

Albert Grass practicing stage magic, undated photograph.

THE PRAYING MANTIS

Year: 1931
Filmmaker: Charmion de Forde
Music: Duke Ellington, "Mooche," "Black and Tan"
Transfer note: copied at 24 frames per second
from a 16mm black-and-white Kodak print with variable density optical sound track
Running time: 6 minutes 24 seconds

By the 1920s the subway had reached Coney Island, inaugurating an era
of great proletarian crowds. It was also the era of Prohibition, and since
the resort was perfectly situated for landing speedboats carrying liquor,
speakeasies sprang up everywhere. The wealthy young people who drove
down to the shore were slumming, looking for kicks. One young socialite
who found her way to Surf Avenue was Charmion de Forde, the daughter
of a successful Wall Street financier. It appears she determined to spend
her trust fund as fast as possible, and cabarets of Coney Island offered
a perfect venue for her experiments in free love. Coney Island had a
reputation for illicit sex dating back at least to the Elephant Hotel built in
1882. The expression "seeing the elephant," accompanied by a grin and a
knowing wink, came to refer to just such pleasures. Patricia White recalls
her great aunt Charmion advising her to, "sleep with a lot of men so when
you meet the right one, you'll know what to do." Miss White added, "it
was rather shocking advice coming from an old lady."

Charmion de Forde was not only wealthy, she was well educated
and saw herself as a "new woman." In the 1920s she studied at Clark
University, where psychoanalysis had been very much in vogue ever since
Freud's lectures here in 1909. It was on this visit, his only trip to the
United States, that Freud visited Coney Island.

It is tempting to think of Charmion as the Peggy Guggenheim of the
Coney Island Amateur Psychoanalytic Society, a rich, rather eccentric
patroness who had numerous affairs. She bought one of the first Cine-
Kodak Motion Picture camera and Kodascope projectors in 1923 and
donated it to the Society. But Charmion was more than just a patroness,
she was also an artist in her own right.

The most interesting question raised by *The Praying Mantis* is whether
Charmion was familiar with the avant-garde. Her film is the only one
made by a member of the society in which one can discern the influence
of surrealist cinema, which was itself deeply influenced by Freud's

theories. Had Charmion visited the Julian Levy gallery for a screening of *Un Chien Andalou*? Her film opens with a close-up of Praying Mantis, a female insect that kills her mate during copulation. This strange image-metaphor would not have been out of place in the work of Luis Buñuel. At the same time this fascination with cruelty and procreation recalls the surrealist nature films of Jean Painlevé.

The other tantalizing clue is the title: "You've been two timing me with Rrose." Was Rrose merely a typo or an allusion to Rrose Sélavy, Duchamp's female alter ego? That the character we have just seen in the film is a man dressed as a woman who very much resembles Man Ray's famous 1921 photograph of Duchamp in drag indicates that this is indeed a reference. That Duchamp coined the name Rrose Sélavy as a pun ("Eros, that's life") would have doubtless delighted Charmion. The very theme of her dream is a wish to manifest her bisexuality.

The film begins with a visit to an older couple. The wife is clearly a man in drag who makes advances to the dreamer. They are referred to in the titles as "Mr. and Mrs. K." Patricia White has suggested that this may have been a reference to the Kennedys. Mr. Kennedy was Charmion's father's business partner. The names may also refer to Herr and Frau K. in Freud's case history of Dora. Did Mr. Kennedy make advances to the teenaged Charmion in the same way that Herr K. pressed his attention on Dora? We may never know. The dream continues with a faked pregnancy and biplane ride over Manhattan. Charmion quotes Freud on how women's dreams of flying are associated with a wish for male sexuality.

In the second half of the film Charmion cuts to what Freud referred to as the "day's residue," or in her case, the night before in one of Coney Island's cabarets, probably the Harvard Inn founded by the gangster Frankie Yale. The film concluded with a scene of Charmion as a young girl making love with a man and another girl, a confession of bisexual desire that underpins the fluid, ever-shifting gender roles in her dream.

That she was able to afford to make a film with optical sound as early as 1931 shows that she had ample financial resources. Sound was a brand-new technology that had only just become standard in cinemas. Her choice of Duke Ellington for the soundtrack suggests that when she wasn't spending her evenings in Coney Island she may have been at the Cotton Club in Harlem.

Opposite: Charmion de Forde (right) and unidentified friend, Glen Cove, Long Island, ca. 1921.

YOWS BUGS THEYS YAMA YAMA GOILS.

THIS IS THE LIFE.

THE BEAR DREAM

Year: 1937
Filmmaker: Arthur Rosenzweig
Transfer note: copied at 18 frames per second
from a 16mm black-and-white Kodak safety film original
Running time: 4 minutes 10 seconds

While Jacob Rosenzweig was the epitome of a successful Jewish businessman who rose from poverty in New York's Lower East Side to become the owner of R & B Furs, Inc., his son, Arthur, conformed to another Jewish archetype, that of the shy scholar.

One could compare *The Bear Dream*, in which Arthur Rosenzweig finds himself transformed into a bear, with Franz Kafka's story *The Metamorphosis*, in which the protagonist is changed into a helpless insect. Like Kafka, Rosenzweig struggled with a domineering father who wanted him to enter the family business. Bob Rosenzweig remembers his uncle Arthur as a wonderful, playful, absentminded professor. Rosenzweig graduated from City College with an MS in Zoology and went on to be a high school science teacher. He pioneered innovative teaching methods. Instead of expecting his students to learn by rote, he encouraged them to make dioramas, take field trips, and collect specimens. Rosenzweig documented his teaching methods for a pilot program funded by Cornell University, incorporating some of the material into *The Bear Dream*.[1]

Rosenzweig dreams he has been transformed into a bear chained up on the roof of the school. His pupils spy on him through a telescope. They find the metamorphosis of their professor hilarious and waste no time spreading the news over the radio. The strange thing is that Arthur finds himself actually enjoying the experience as a group of young women surround him, petting and fondling his big fur coat and feeding him snacks. He is afraid that if they find out who is really underneath all that fur, they might stop their loving. In the second half of the film Rosenzweig analyzes his dream. He concludes that it expresses a repressed desire for sexual relations with one of his students, Dorothy, and that the bear skin fulfills the same function as the young man's overcoat in a dream analyzed by Freud, which signified that he was afraid that a condom would break and lead to an unfortunate pregnancy.[2]

He also links the figure of a bear-man to his first feelings of sexual arousal experienced when his father took him to Coney Island freak shows as a young teenager. He was excited by the risqué and exotic young women who would pretend to be half animal. Roberta Leviton describes

Left: Arthur Rosenzweig always carried this picture of his student Dorothy in his wallet. Right: Arthur Rosenzweig at his parents' home in Forest Hills, Queens, undated.

one such spectacle: "All along the Bowery and Surf Avenue, Coney's ballyhoo spielers plied their art on potential customers, 'Come right in, ladies and gents. Come in and see Koo Koo, the bird girl—she's half bird and half woman—pos-i-tively alive. Born without teeth or gums. Don't expect to see her flying around inside when you go in. Koo Koo's half bird but she don't fly. But she puts all her little bird soul into making people laugh. If you don't laugh yourself sick when you see her dancin' the Charleston, you better go out and get a couple of doctors.'"[3]

Oddly Arthur Rosenzweig never mentions that the bear might conjure up Oedipal rivalry for the affections of the opposite sex. His father, Jacob, was after all in the fur business. Bob recalls that his great uncle could well have been described a great "bear of a man" with a booming voice. His bear hugs could practically knock one off one's feet. Only in his dream could Arthur usurp the patriarch, surrounding himself with a harem of women. Perhaps it was something that he simply could not imagine in his waking life.

Notes

1. Written notes for the educational film and sections of the complete film with intertitles were found in the archive.
2. Sigmund Freud, *The Interpretation of Dreams*, trans. A. A. Brill (New York: Barnes and Noble, 2005), 163.
3. Roberta Leviton, "Cardboard Paradise: The Story of Coney Island," unpublished manuscript, Archives and Special Collections Division, Brooklyn College, CUNY, 19.

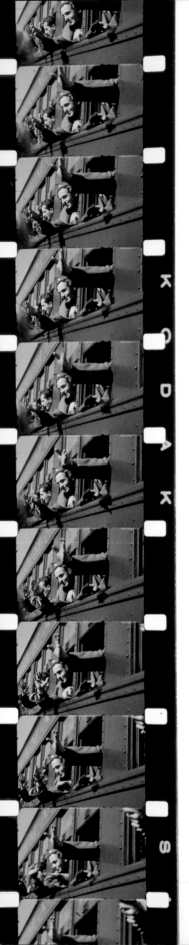

Chasing Louis Schnekowitz

Year: 1945
Filmmaker: Molly Lippman
Transfer note: copied at 18 frames per second
from a Regular 8mm black-and-white Kodak film and Regular 8mm Kodachrome original
Running time: 3 minutes 50 seconds

Robert Troutman, a younger member of the Coney Island Amateur Psychoanalytic Society, remembers Molly Lippman vividly from the mid-1960s. He adored her. As a gay man, he found she was one person in whom he could confide and who accepted him for who he was. Molly would drop in regularly to meetings of the Society as she had for the past twenty years. She was a large lady with flaming red hair who spoke her mind. City Council members called her "Marching Molly" or, less kindly, "The Brooklyn Battle Axe" or "The Floral Firecracker," referring to the loud floral prints that she loved to wear.

She told Robert stories of her first experiences of Coney Island. Her family were summer renters who came down from the Bronx. On hot nights, she and her three sisters would sleep on the beach or the fire escape. She remembered, "After supper, we'd sit out all night on the porch. We'd bring down food to share with the neighbors. Coney Island was a real summer resort as designed by nature, for all the people to enjoy, regardless of race, color, or creed. In those days, it was a different world—not like nowadays. Even the weather seemed different. People were more apt to be people." Her family returned to the same cramped complex bungalow every year as did all the other families.

She recalled how the Depression hit Coney Island hard. As a young girl she listened to Socialists and Communists giving street-corner speeches about how the government could help the poor. She watched as Harry Zarch, who owned a moving company on West 27th Street, helped needy Coney Islanders, cruising up and down the streets in his moving van, and whenever he saw an evicted family, he gathered up their belongings and moved them into cottages he owned.

She couldn't afford to go to college full time. During the day she worked in accounts payable at the office of G & B Furs, Inc., while taking evening classes at City College. Marx and Freud were her heroes. She saw psychoanalysis very much the same way that she understood socialism as a path for the emancipation of working people. Just as wages

Molly Lippman in an attic she shared with Lois Gropman, ca. 1940.

and proper housing were necessary for the body, so would psychoanalysis free the mind from superstition and sexual prudery.

The subject of her film was a dream about another member of the Society, Louis Schnekowitz, who had enlisted in the army. In her dream she tries desperately to catch up with Louis before he is shipped off to Europe to fight in World War II. On awakening she remembers that she had spent the day fending off her employer, who was teasing her about when she was going to get married. Her analysis shows that, while the manifest content of the dream revolved around a fear that Louis would die in battle, her latent wish was that Louis would propose. She was afraid that she would lose him not to the Germans but to another woman.

Molly had met Louis in Coney Island. He was stationed at Seagate barracks within walking distance of the amusement park. The war was definitely taking a toll on the neighborhood. Molly recalled that in 1942 air raid wardens started patrolling the streets. Steeplechase had to close when darkness fell. Long stretches of the boardwalk were plunged into utter darkness. Everyone became very patriotic. Shooting galleries added new wartime targets; patrons aimed fake machine guns at German parachutists as barkers screamed, "Nail the Nazi before he lands!" Louis couldn't pass one by without stopping to test his marksmanship.

Though she did ultimately lose Louis to another woman, Molly remained fiercely loyal to Coney Island. After graduating from college, she got a job at the Coney Island Chamber of Commerce. It was at this time that Robert Moses, the Parks Commissioner, started cracking down. He hated the raucous and fun-loving amusement zone and was determined to turn it into a subdued area of public parks and apartment complexes. As a community organizer, Molly fought him every step of the way. She also campaigned for women's rights and more day-care centers in the community and became a great friend of another early feminist in politics, Bella Abzug.

A psychoanalytic interpretation might stress her fight to save the neighborhood could be interpreted as a transference of her love for Louis. She never did marry. After a long battle with arthritis, she died at age ninety at Coney Island Hospital on Ocean Parkway in 1990.

Molly Lippman reading to her grandnephew, Benny, 1965.

THE LION DREAM

Year: 1947
Filmmaker: Teddy Weisengrund
Transfer note: copied at 18 frames per second from a 16mm black-and-white
Kodak safety film original and an Agfa black-and-white 16mm print
Running time: 2 minutes 47 seconds

Teddy Weisengrund was the only member of the Coney Island Amateur Psychoanalytic Society to become a practicing analyst. Robert Troutman recalls that members of the Society would evoke his name with great pride. However, after he moved to San Diego, Weisengrund appears to have severed all ties with his former friends. Perhaps he felt that his days as an amateur might mar his professional credentials.

Weisengrund grew up in the heady atmosphere of the Weimar Republic. We catch a glimpse of his childhood from *The Lion Dream*, which Weisengrund compiled in the late 1940s from home movies shot by his parents some fifteen years earlier. He was the only child of Jewish intellectuals. His father, Wilhelm Weisengrund,[1] appears to have been a minor member of the Frankfurt School who contributed an essay on leisure activities of the working classes to Max Horkheimer's *Zeitschrift für Sozialwissenschaft*. His aunt Lisle, also seen in the film, was a psychoanalyst and follower of Melanie Klein.

In *The Lion Dream* we meet young Teddy, a troubled, even neurotic, three year old. Doubtless he must have picked up on his parents' anxiety. Too young to understand the real threat of National Socialism, he feared attack by lions. In the film, Weisengrund includes some horrifying footage of lions eating their prey from a 1930s 16mm German film. This suggests that he saw those images not in the cinema, as he claims, but in his own home on the family projector. Weisengrund's film shows how he unconsciously blamed himself for his inability, even as a small child, to rescue his family from the concentration camps.

Unable to obtain work abroad, Wilhelm Weisengrund could not leave Germany. He sent his only son, alone, to live with a distant relative, Manny Mintz, in Coney Island. The large and rambunctious Mintz family was already crammed into an apartment above Kirschner's Drugs on Mermaid Avenue. Mr. Mintz owned an old-fashioned photo studio on Surf Avenue. He used a large wooden-cased camera and had lots of props where holidaymakers could stick their heads through wooden cutouts of

comic-book characters, gorillas, and bikini-clad girls or be photographed against painted backdrops.

Jews had been moving into Coney Island in large numbers, particularly west of Twentieth Street, which became known as the "shtetl by the sea." Some of them helped sponsor European refugees who settled in the area. On every street corner phonographs played the refugee refrain *Wie Ahien Sol Ich Gehn?* (Where Shall I Go?) Though Teddy moved into a Jewish neighborhood, he must have felt estranged and lonely. He came from an assimilated intellectual family. Singing Yiddish songs on the boardwalk with the Mintzes and their friends was quite foreign to him. In fact he didn't know any Yiddish. Nor did he speak English. It was quite possible that Manny Mintz wasn't really a relative at all, just a kind man who wanted to help a Jewish child from Germany.

Note
1. He should not be confused with the philosopher and sociologist Theodor W. Adorno, who changed his name from Wiesengrund to Adorno when he emigrated to the United States in the 1930s.

Further Reading: The short story "A Day in Coney Island" in *The Collected Stories of Isaac Bashevis Singer* (New York: Farrar, Straus & Giroux, 1982) is an evocative firsthand account of Jewish refugee culture in Coney Island shortly before the outbreak of war.

THE LONELY CHICKEN DREAM

Year: 1954
Filmmaker: Beverly d'Angelo
Transfer note: copied at 24 frames per second
from a 16mm Kodachrome original with magnetic stripped sound
Sound: from the album *Wild Percussion and Horns A' Plenty*,
Dick Schory's New Percussion Ensemble
Running time: 3 minutes

Beverly d'Angelo née Baladamenti came from an old Coney Island family.
It is probable that the Baladamenti family originally emigrated from
Sicily in the late nineteenth century. Mrs. d'Angelo's uncle Vinny was a
clown and later a pitchman in Luna Park in the 1930s and into the 1940s.
Her father was a cook at Gargiulo's restaurant, a neighborhood landmark
that opened its doors in 1907 and continues to this day. He loved to tell
her about all the famous customers he had served, the gangsters who used
to eat here in the 1930s: Frankie Yale, Al Capone, and their buddies; as
well as politicians like Fiorello La Guardia and Robert Moses.

By the 1940s Coney was no longer the glittering showplace it had
been a half century earlier. This was the era of "The Poor Man's Riviera."
Steeplechase Park and the Cyclone, seen in *The Lonely Chicken Dream*,
continued to operate, but the luxury hotels, ballrooms, music halls, and
cabarets had disappeared. Beverly liked to quote her father: "We used to
cater to the classes. Now we cater to the masses."

Robert Troutman saw Mrs. d'Angelo once in a while in the early
1960s when she drove down from Long Island for meetings in a powder
blue Corvette. He told me that she seemed the least likely member of the
Society to be intellectually captivated by psychoanalysis. A working-class
Brooklyn woman, she had married a man named Buster when she was
eighteen and had several children. Starting out as a laundry deliveryman,
Buster d'Angelo had done well, and by the early 1950s had moved his
family to New Hyde Park. He was a passionate amateur movie maker
with all the latest equipment. When he was not shooting home movies, he
spent most of his leisure time with his buddies at Belmont or Roosevelt
Raceway in Westbury, leaving his wife alone for long periods of time.
Troutman confided to me that he suspected Buster may have had ties to
organized crime, but Beverly simply told people that he was a contractor.

Above left: Beverly d'Angelo's uncle Ugo and aunt Theresa Gaspanella, Coney Island, undated. Theresa gave palm readings on the Bowery.
Above right: Beverly d'Angelo's uncle, Vittorio (Vinny) Baladamenti, undated. During the 1930s and 1940s Vinny was a clown and later a pitchman in Luna Park.
Opposite: Beverly d'Angelo, 1954, photograph by Gray Studios, Long Island N.Y.

It is clear from *The Lonely Chicken Dream* that Mrs. d'Angelo felt isolated in the suburbs. She suspected Buster of having an affair with a younger woman named Betty. She longed to go back in time to her carefree childhood in Coney Island. She developed insomnia and headaches. Troutman's diagnosis: Beverly was suffering from a case of what Freud dubbed "housewife's neurosis" or a sociologist would call "anomie," suburban alienation. Apparently she understood psychoanalysis as a kind of self-help therapy. Though she herself had no idea how to shoot a film, she confided to Troutman that she secretly cut up her husband's home movie to create her dream films. *The Lonely Chicken Dream* shows just how successful and subversive her strategy was, as she replaced Buster's vision with her own.

THE ABANDONED ARK

Year: 1962
Filmmaker: Stella Weiss
Transfer note: copied at 18 frames per second
from 16mm black-and-white Kodak safety film and Kodachrome Regular 8mm
Running time: 4 minutes 16 seconds

Robert Troutman remembers that Stella Weiss had all the makings of a Borscht Belt comedienne, a sharp wit and keen eye for the foibles of her Jewish friends. It wasn't always clear whether what she said was meant to be taken straight or satirically. Was her dream film really all about her guilt over her failure as a Jewish mother or was she privately sending up the whole stereotype of the "Jewish mother": long suffering, overprotective, self-sacrificing, and intent on stuffing her children full of food? Perhaps both of these ideas are present in *The Abandoned Ark*, where Stella dreams that she is about to sail away in a rickety old ark, forgetting her young son and daughter who are left behind to scavenge on the beach amidst garbage and chickens.

The ark in the dream references not only the ark of the Old Testament but its sideshow incarnation in Coney Island's Luna Park. Built in 1914, this ark was filled with toys of every description, including stuffed cats, dogs, sheep, and various sorts of tin toys. Noah himself dispensed the gifts to children.[1] Stella would have been familiar with it as a young child. In her analysis of the dream, Stella discusses how difficult it was for her to turn down her children's requests for toys and treats that she couldn't afford. We see them looking in the store windows on Mermaid Avenue. Thus she images herself inside an ark that is nothing but an empty shell.

By 1962, the date of Stella's dream, Coney Island's ark was no more than a memory. Luna Park closed in 1946. Yet the idea had contemporary relevance. This was the height of the Cuban Missile Crisis, when many Americans feared their world might at any moment be annihilated by nuclear warfare. The desolate landscape of the dream hints at this. At the same time, one might speculate that for Stella, personally, the ark signified a new beginning, a wish that she could sail away and start over again, as carefree as her children Shirley and Danny, who are included in the film as teenagers accompanied by the inter-title, "Not a care in the World. I should have been so lucky when I was their age." Following a darker chain of Freudian associations, one might link the ark to Stella's

Stella Weiss (far left) in the records department of Edo Aircraft Corporation during World War II.

body, a ruined womb, a watery grave, a floating coffin, wasting away rather than setting out to sea. On the side of life or death, the symbolism of the ark remains ambiguous.

Like another member of the Society, Molly Lippman, Stella and her family rented a bungalow every summer in Coney Island in the early 1940s. But while Molly remembers those summers fondly as a time of camaraderie and good cheer, Stella recalls the cramped quarters and the nosy neighbors, a place without privacy where late-night arguments between socialists and communists could keep one from getting a night's sleep.

During World War II Stella worked in the records department of Edo Aircraft Corporation. After the war, her husband's business in machine parts prospered and she didn't have to work, but she always envied those who had a higher education, and she loved to attend lectures at the local library. By the early 1960s they had a country house near Mahopac, New York. They could afford to send their children to college but much to Stella's disappointment, they had turned into a couple of "beatniks" and had little time for formal education. Perhaps Stella felt that here too, as a mother, she had failed to inspire her children with a love of learning.

Note
1. "Dancing the Thing at Coney Island," *New York Times*, May 31, 1914, page C5.

My Dream of Dental Irritation

Year: 1964
Filmmaker: Robert Troutman "Bobby Beaujolais"
Transfer note: copied at 18 frames per second from an 8mm Kodachrome camera original with magnetic stripped sound
Music: "The Man That Got Away" and "Somewhere over the Rainbow," sung by Judy Garland on the album *Judy at Carnegie Hall*
Running time: 5 minutes 9 seconds

Robert Troutman grew up in the Coney Island Houses, the first of the large-scale high-rise projects that were built under the auspices of Robert Moses. His father, Joe, was a World War II veteran. He had served in the Fifth Army and swam ashore at Anzio Beach in Italy in 1944. Joe Troutman left the family when his son was eight years old. Robert remembers him yelling at his mother, blaming her for his "sissy" son. He loved his mother dearly and confided that he was secretly happy when his father left the two of them alone.

From a very early age Robert Troutman felt different. He didn't want to play with the other boys. Instead, he liked to visit Mrs. Adler next door. She sewed costumes for the Laughing Lady in one of the dark tunnels. He remembers sitting at her feet watching her work, picking out the sparkly trimmings.

As a teenager, Robert Troutman started spending time at The World in Wax Musée.[1] Sometimes he'd hold perfectly still, pretending to be a waxwork, until one of the older men who frequented the museum started inspecting him closely. Then he'd bat his eyelashes and give him a special smile. Sometimes the owner, Lillie Santangelo, would let him spruce up one of the waxworks, do their hair and makeup, add some red paint to one of the more grisly murders on display. Troutman loved to draw and paint and soon started earning money painting signs for many of the sideshows. It was the start of a career. In the early 1960s, Troutman got a break working in the art department of a large Madison Avenue advertising firm. The opening titles of his film *My Dream of Dental Irritation* show his skill in commercial design.

Troutman says he was drawn to the Coney Island Amateur Psychoanalytic Society as a teenager struggling to come to terms with his homosexuality. As he put it, "at least there, sex wasn't a dirty word. Freud never said that people like me were sick." It was here that he first

Robert Troutman, in his first theatrical appearance, 1951. He plays an Egyptian prince (far right) appealing to King Herod.

"came out." In his film, Troutman dreams that he and another young man pull out their dentures. In his analysis he draws on a similar dream analyzed by Freud in which a young homosexual dreams of watching an opera with someone he desires, then flies across the floor and pulls out two teeth. In reality he had been "thrown down"—rejected by other men—and now he is afraid it might happen again. He confesses that after his last rejection, he masturbated anyway. Freud explains that the not uncommon dream of dental irritation or losing one's teeth signifies a transference from the genital region to the face as symbols of unconscious thought. In dreams lips refer to the clitoris, the nose the penis, and the cheeks the buttocks.[2]

Troutman dreams not of the opera but of a place that he knew much better, Club Elegante at 1060 Ocean Parkway.[3] He follows this scene with a brief shot of a large billboard of a man blowing smoke rings, this "blow job" cutting to the very phallic Empire State Building. After he analyzes his dream, explaining how it signifies desire for a young man who had rejected him, Troutman ends with a coda. It is a short yet touching

THE BOBSLED

Year: 1972
Filmmaker: Eddie Kammerer
Transfer note: copied at 24 frames per second from a 16mm black-and-white Kodak reversal camera original and Kodachrome camera original with magnetic stripped sound
Music: "Sisters of Mercy" by Leonard Cohen
Running time: 2 minutes 25 seconds

Like Teddy Weisengrund, Eddie Kammerer did not shoot original footage to illustrate his dream. Instead, he edited childhood home movies shot by his parents twenty years earlier. He tells the story by recutting the footage and adding inter-titles and music of his own era, the 1970s.

His film depicts a recurring nightmare. Kammerer is a child again, desperately searching for his mother. He believes he must find her before she goes riding on the Bobsled, where she will surely die in a horrible accident.[1] He always finds her at the very moment her little car shoots down the slope. At this point he wakes up. Kammerer then shows how his dream centers on his desire to see his mother again; at the same time he blames himself for the fact that she ran away with her lover, abandoning young Eddie and his father.

There is something obsessive and dark about Kammerer's depiction of Coney Island accentuated by the dingy gray black-and-white photography. Steeplechase Park seems grim. Mrs. Kammerer stares blackly into the funhouse mirror as her husband stands next to her with his camera on a tripod, reflecting a loveless marriage. The color film shot by Mrs. Kammerer of her son and lover, Frank, is more cheerful, but nonetheless it is clear that Eddie was a troubled child. After she left, Eddie and his father moved out of Coney in the late 1950s as welfare recipients were moved in. His father had grown bitter, and the neighborhood was changing for the worse.

Robert Troutman remembers Kammerer, who was several years younger than him, as a withdrawn, moody hippie who wandered back to Coney Island with his guitar. "He had his demons. For him Coney Island was haunted by his mother, forever young and beautiful and out of reach," Troutman recalls. "He took the Amateur Psychoanalytic Society very seriously. He really thought Freudian analysis might help him, but later he got into Easter philosophy and kind of drifted away." Troutman also recalled that Kammerer didn't bathe very often. The gradual destruction of Coney Island didn't surprise Kammerer. "It was as if it was an externalization of all the anger and disappointment that he had stored up over the years."

Eddie Kammerer at home with his girlfriend, Tracy Reynolds, and their new baby, Cassidy, 1972.

The 1970s, when Kammerer made his film, was indeed a dark decade for Coney Island. There were fires almost every day. Steeplechase Park had been demolished in 1966 by Fred C. Trump, Donald Trump's father. In 1974 the Bobsled was torn down. And in 1975 health officials shut down the riding stables in Steeplechase Park because of filthy and hazardous conditions. Those ponies had delighted children for generations. We can see them in Teddy Weisengrund's film where a blond little boy on a dappled pony reminded him of playing on a rocking horse. In *The Bobsled* we see Eddie riding around the track.

Note

1. The Bobsled was first seen at the 1939 World's Fair in Flushing Meadows. Joe Bonsignore bought it when the fair closed and brought it to Coney Island. He installed it on the site of the old Staunch's Dance Hall at the Bowery and Stillwell Avenue. It was always a dangerous ride, which was maintained by Joe's son John Bonsignore, the engineer of the family. Finally in the late 1950s a minor accident did happen. John remembers how every night he'd "wake up in a cold sweat dreaming that the ride was out of control, 'I was in shock. I had those crazy dreams and would wake up reliving the accident.'" (*Wild Ride!: A Coney Island Roller Coaster Family* by Charles Denson, p. 93.)

pages 100–103: The Coney Island World in Wax Musée tableaux. "John Roche murdering a girl on her way to school"; "John Christie, the Full Moon Strangler and Victim"; "Lina Medina, the Five-Year-Old Mother." Photographs by Costa Mantis taken shortly before the museum closed in 1981.

Lina MEDINA

caso extraordinario
a ciencia medica.
s cinco anos de edad
o un hijo. sesenta
tores aten dieron su
ecera logrando el
to por operacion
area. actualmente
toda una señora
bajando como secretaria
su patria. Peru. Su Hijo
odo un hombre.

BABY BOYS MOTHER IS BABY TOO

LINA MEDINA is 5 years old. thirty seven inches tall has her first teeth. but thats her baby son nurse is holding at LIMA PERU hospital. as baby's mother gazes stodidly from bed. Infant weighed almost six pounds at ceasarean birth. SIXTY DOCTORS WATCHED STRANGE EVENT.

PRIMAL SCENES: SIGMUND FREUD, CONEY ISLAND, AND THE STAGING OF DOMESTIC TRAUMA

Amy Herzog

We're all only kids grown tall, and everything is right with us
unless we've got tuberculosis of the heart.
—Fred Thompson, creator of Luna Park

The wish manifested in the dream must be an infantile one....
Dreamland will resemble a nursery, the world of the child.
—Albert Grass, Coney Island Amateur Psychoanalytic Society

In the dream life, the child, as it were, continues his existence in the man,
with a retention of all his traits and wishes, including those which he was obliged
to allow to fall into disuse in his later years. With irresistible might it will be
impressed on you by what processes of development, of repression, sublimation and
reaction there arises out of the child, with its peculiar gifts and tendencies, the so-called
normal man, the bearer and partly the victim of our painfully acquired civilization.
—Sigmund Freud, lectures at Clark University, 1909

Sigmund Freud's 1909 trip to the United States was a momentous one. Freud and Carl Jung were set to deliver a series of influential lectures at Clark University, where they would each receive honorary degrees; their talks would introduce the practice of psychoanalysis for the first time before an American audience. Though delivered in German, Freud's lectures generated a huge amount of controversy, reshaping the field of psychiatry in the U.S. and securing Freud's position on an international stage. While Freud did not reference his visit to Coney Island directly in these lectures, one cannot help but to wonder what points of resonance Freud might have found between his pending talks on infantile sexuality

Opposite: Entrance to the Coney Island Baby Incubators exhibit, undated photograph.

and repressed desire and the spectacles of excess and eternal juvenilia that greeted him within the gates of Dreamland.

Indeed, there are a number of clear and compelling links between the man and the park, as well as some rather pleasurable contradictions. Certainly the image of the stately doctor adrift in a plaster wonderland is difficult to resist, the scholar of repression suddenly confronted with a gaudy display of unrepentant pleasure, burbling with vice and sexuality beneath the surface. Regardless of Freud's personal reactions to the park (as documented in Norman Klein's contribution to this collection), however, it might prove even more productive to compare the larger thrust of his psychoanalytic project with the modus operandi of Coney Island. In what ways might the operational logic of Coney Island cohere or diverge from Freudian theory? Might Coney Island exist, in fact, as a distinctly Freudian space? My project in this essay will be to explore some of the points of connection and dissonance between Freud's theories and the amusements offered for consumption at Coney Island's various attractions and parks. Of particular interest will be the spectacles of domesticity, and of domestic trauma, that have continually resurfaced throughout Coney Island's history.

Viewed as a carnival of wish fulfillment, the collective desires and fears on display at Coney Island correlate with those documented in Freud's case files. In both we find evidence of acute anxiety regarding sexuality, shifting gender roles, and the impact of familial relations on the development of the self, particularly as these issues are compounded by the onset of modernity and new technologies. Yet while Coney Island might have served as an extravagant exhibition of the kinds of symptoms and neurosis to which Freud devoted his study, the guiding principles of the park could not be further from the object of Freudian psychoanalysis.

As a spectacle, Coney Island is perhaps more in line with the showmanship of a practitioner like Freud's early mentor, Jean-Martin Charcot. Charcot was a neurologist who worked with a large number of patients suffering from hysteria at the Salpêtrière hospital in France. Freud was particularly influenced by Charcot's observation that a "nervous shock" or trauma could act as a trigger, unleashing a disproportionately severe series of debilitating symptoms. Charcot remained convinced that hysteria was facilitated by a neurological weakness, however, and set out to observe systematically the physical manifestations of hysteria. He used hypnosis to induce patients to perform

Postcard, Creation Entrance, Dreamland, Coney Island, ca. 1909.

their ailments, including spasms, seizures, and contorted postures for the educational benefit of his students. These sessions proved to be incredibly captivating, theatrical events, and they soon evolved into celebrated weekly public displays for large audiences of scientists, politicians, writers, visiting dignitaries, and artists. Charcot famously photographed the most spectacular of these hysterical performances in an attempt to observe more precisely their physical nuances, in particular the gesticulations of costumed female patients striking "attitudes passionnelles," theatrical and often eroticized poses of extreme emotional states.[1] Similarly Coney Island subscribed to the method of creating elaborate visual icons, surface-level expressions of interior states put on display with little incentive for self-realization.

Freud's 1909 lectures patiently outlined the methodology of psychoanalysis: suggestions presented by analyst act as a catalyst for the analysand, who performs acts of mental work, confronting her own blockages and transforming her mental system into a healthier balance. Coney Island is not about balance or resolution or cure—it appears to prefer reveling in the spectacular pleasures of its base "surrogate symptoms."

Postcard, undated. A sweeping view of Tozman Plaza in Midget City, which looks identical to any "full-size" town when photographed with only its inhabitants.

Indeed, Coney Island's turn-of-the-century iconography might have been read as both a confirmation and an elaborate mockery of the crisis Freud was to face in the New World. At the time of the Clark lectures, Freud was on the cusp of a series of rifts with Jung and Clark University President G. Stanley Hall over what they saw as his single-minded fixation on sexuality. American psychologists, such as those in the audience for the Clark talks, tended to be resistant to discussions of sexuality, and Freud's frank commentary generated heated discussions in the field. In light of this controversy, it is tempting to read the fecund female thighs and breasts that towered over the entrance to Dreamland in 1909 as both an affirmation of Freud's contention that sexuality is central to human psychology and as a talisman for his own irrepressible and inconvenient obsessions. Coney Island might function, in fact, as a kind of untrained, adolescent, rogue analyst, one who guides the analysand through a series of repetitive revelations that do little more than to feed the flames of his pathological symptoms.

EXHIBITIONISM, DOMESTICITY, AND TRAUMA

Much has been written about Coney Island and the spectacularization of trauma. Particularly during the time of Freud's visit, the various

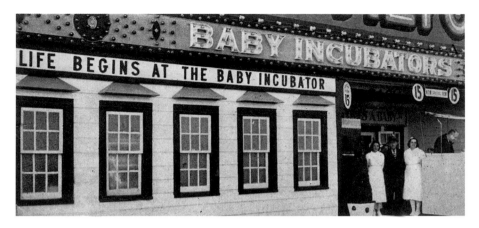

"Baby Incubators," Coney Island, ca. 1950.

parks at the resort were rife with depictions of Heaven and Hell, disaster
spectacles culled from literary and travel texts, and—most dramatic—
large-scale reenactments of floods and fires. Exhibitions such as "Fire
and Flames" at Luna Park and "The Fall of Pompei" at Dreamland seem
clear manifestations of the death instinct, attainable for endless repetition
for the mere purchase of a ticket.

A surprisingly large number of attractions at Dreamland and Luna
Park, however, took as their objects the banal practices of everyday
life. Sandwiched between the bizarre and the exotic were displays of a
far more domestic order, albeit in each case with some fantastic twist.
The village of Lilliputia presented a miniaturized but fully functional
community inhabited by persons with dwarfism and others of short
stature. Persons from foreign countries were similarly put on display
in "native villages," where visitors could view them as they went about
their daily activities. And Dreamland and Luna Park each had long-
running exhibitions of live incubator babies, prematurely born children
held in mechanically controlled environments, under the supervision
of Dr. Martin Couney and a team of wet nurses who fed the babies
with tubes and nasal spoons (in a rather un–Coney Islandesque move,
Dr. Couney prohibited the wet nurses from eating hot dogs).[2] Babies
who otherwise had little chance for survival were offered treatment
via incubator through the exhibitions at a time when hospitals were
reticent to embrace the new technology. In exchange, the babies' care

was offered for public viewing until the children were viable. In each of these examples, the monotonous tasks of daily existence are rendered strange through difference (physiological, ethnic, medical/technological). Exoticism, exhibitionism, exploitation, and utopian fantasies collide with the realities of living; in each of the exhibitions cited above, the residents of these displays inhabited them full-time, forging real lives and communities that carried on after the last visitors had gone home for the night.

If Coney Island is the playground of eternal childhood, it seems somewhat natural that its adolescent fantasies of strange locales and thrilling adventures would be juxtaposed with attractions rooted in the psychopathology of the everyday. This contradiction provides the most salient point of intersection between the design of Coney Island and the writings of Sigmund Freud. The persistent child, who has been brutally repressed within "adult," civilized society, can nearly always be unleashed with a bit of prodding. Whether for entertainment or for treatment, however, this unleashing invariably poses certain risks and reveals the potential flaws and illnesses wrought by suppression.

Freud defined the "primal scene," in a clinical sense, as the traumatic exposure of the child to his parents engaged in sexual intercourse. Freud himself is not always clear as to whether this scene is actually experienced by the child, or if the scene is in fact the child's fantasy. Contemporary scholars have questioned the universality of this scenario, citing a diverse range of familial relationships, degrees of exposure, and preexisting anxieties as factors that might impact the blow of a primal encounter.[3] I would like to propose a more porous definition of the primal scene, linking it to any formative, irresolvable trauma that serves, for the individual, as a nexus of self-definition and as an image that is continually replayed. Primal images, I would argue, can function on a collective register; one need only look to the endless looping of disaster footage or child-murderers on cable news channels to find ample evidence of collective primal trauma. Yet the parameters of collective primal imagery are relatively fixed: the crimes that captivate us most tend to be those that take place in or around the home. We witness a betrayal of familial roles and responsibilities. And within the collective primal scene, we are often confronted with sadistic, "unnatural" sexual acts.

While domestic or familial-themed amusements might not be the most prominent of Coney Island's offerings, they are among the most surreal

and uncanny sights to be found at the resort, primal displays with a
distinctly Freudian legacy.

THE WORLD IN WAX
No exhibition devoted itself more fully to the celebration of domestic
trauma than Lillie Beatrice Santangelo's World in Wax Musée. First
opened in 1926, the Wax Musée featured a parade of celebrities and heads
of state immortalized in life-size wax portraits. While these displays
remained a mainstay of the museum for more than five decades, a large
portion of the institution was dedicated to dioramas of familial violence,
serial killers caught in the act, and the participants in famous "freak
births." Santangelo's Wax Musée followed in the tradition of waxworks
across North America and, like other wax exhibitions at Coney Island,
paid considerable attention to the re-creation of criminal acts. A visitor
to the Eden Musée at Coney Island (open from 1915–1932) recalled that
"people loved to see the chief moment of a crime reenacted."[4] And with
the proliferation of photography and other visual media, wax museum
operators faced mounting pressure to achieve visual accuracy in the staging
of highly publicized crimes. In a "Talk of the Town" entry about a 1931 trip
to Coney Island, E. B. White observed the increasing costs incurred by the
wax industry: "there was a time when last year's murderess could be turned
into this year's murderess with a few deft strokes; but people nowadays are
so familiar with the appearance of their favorite criminals that brand-new
wax figures have to be made, to insure perfect likenesses."[5]

The crime-scene dioramas and freakish corporeal displays of the wax
museum are in many ways consistent with Coney Island's fascination
with trauma in the public sphere. Yet while the visualization of these
incidents was highly sensationalized, a large degree of their affective
power arises from their placement within banal domestic settings. One of
the most striking aspects of these displays is their continual focus on the
occurrence of crime and abnormality in private spaces and at times within
the family circle. The thrill of the wax museum diorama may stem from
its ability to bring to light events that did, or ought to, take place behind
closed doors.

In one display, for example, William Edward Hickman, "The Fox," is
depicted at work on his twelve-year-old victim, Marion Parker. In 1927
Hickman kidnapped Parker, the daughter of his former employer. Upon
receiving a ransom payment, Hickman sped away from the scene and

William Edward Hickman, "The Fox," at work on his twelve-year-old victim, Marion Parker, Coney Island World in Wax Musée. Photograph by Costa Mantis, 1981.

threw the girl's corpse out of his car; her arms and legs had been cut off, her internal organs had been removed, and her eyes had been wired open so that she would appear alive when viewed through the car window.[6] Rather than displaying the gruesome moment of Parker's return, however, Santangelo's exhibit visualizes a scene that Hickman apparently described during his trial, when he dismembered Parker's body in a hotel bathtub. Memorialized in wax, we see Hickman splayed over the tub, leering at his tiny victim, his bloody arm and knife poised above her limbless, crimson body. Blood pools around Parker's eyes, which remain wide open, confronting the visage of her killer (evidence suggests Parker remained at least semiconscious throughout this mutilation).[7]

The overall impact of the scene, however, is dictated by its staging. The bathroom is cramped and characterless with white tiles and institutional fixtures. Hickman is dressed innocuously in a tightly buttoned pink-striped shirt with plain black slacks; although young (he was only nineteen at the time of the murder), his hairline is receding and his scalp is visible through the thinning strands. Indeed, this scene could

Fred Thompson, a British dishwasher and alcoholic, contemplating the murder of Edith Kiecorius. Coney Island World in Wax Musée. Photograph by Costa Mantis, 1981.

be mistaken at first glance for the benign image of a father bathing his child—that is, until one sees the spattered blood and the missing limbs. This slippage between the familiar and the horrific might also be read in reverse. Hickman's body, with out-thrust arms, looms too large within the tiny, three-walled room. His pose is stiff and unnatural, hovering at an awkward distance from the tub, his left arm turned at an impossible angle. The blocking alone in this display renders the whole genre of parental bath-time scenes perverse and violent. Even without the blood and the explanatory text, one would almost surely get the sense that things in this room have gone terribly wrong.

Our sense that something is amiss is surely heightened by the screen of chicken wire and wooden slats separating museum patrons from the exhibit. Many of the displays in the Wax Musée were framed in this manner, creating the (presumably inadvertent) impression of a cordoned crime scene. In one ambiguous exhibit, Fred Thompson, a middle-aged man, is seated in a small, spare room, listening intently, it seems, to a Bakelite radio. A women's fashion magazine and an aqua plate (or ashtray)

Julio Ramirez Perez, "the Screwdriver Killer," plunges the instrument into his victim's neck. Coney Island World in Wax Musée. Photograph by Costa Mantis, 1981.

rest next to him on a quilt-covered bed; an orange plastic cup is set on the dresser. The bottom third of the exhibit window is blocked by a wire screen and plywood. A newspaper clipping hangs above this barrier: "Girl's Slayer Ruled Insane, Cheats Chair."

In February 1961 fifty-nine-year-old Fred Thompson lured Edith Kiecorius, four, into his rented room in a Chelsea tenement, where he raped and killed her. He was tracked down several days later, living in a trailer on a chicken farm where he had been hired as a laborer. Thompson, a U.K.-born dishwasher and alcoholic, was declared insane and was institutionalized for the rest of his life. It is unclear in photos of the display which moment in Thompson's life we are witnessing: The man at rest within his rented room, contemplating a future crime? His tense hideout on the farm, awaiting capture? The eternal drudgery of self-reflection that Thompson would face in the asylum? The drama that exists here rests in what we know happened rather than in what we see. We are forced to confront the rapist and killer at rest, embalmed in his utter ordinariness. The blankness of Thompson's stare resists

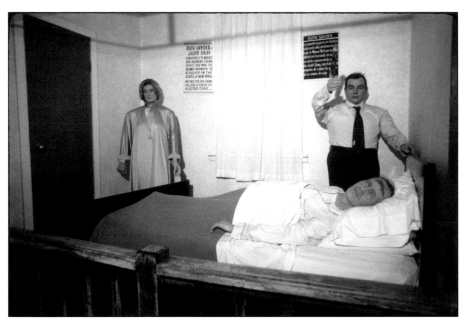

Ruth Snyder and her lover Judd Gray, poised to strike her husband. Coney Island World in Wax Musée. Photograph by Costa Mantis, 1981.

interpretation, yet the framing invites us inside to imagine the goings-on within his troubled, psychic interior, enclosed in his room/cage.

Other displays similarly counterpose the banal with the extreme in a reflective manner. Perhaps it is the requisite stillness of the wax display, but the frozen actions of the figures suggest that we might similarly halt the hands of time and enter into the mind-sets of the participants. Julio Ramirez Perez is caught with a screwdriver plunged into the neck of his victim, Mrs. Vera Lotito, in her apartment. In 1948 Lotito had the misfortune of surprising Perez as he burgled her home, but in the display case of the Wax Musée, it is Perez who seems surprised by the image of his own face reflected in a vanity mirror.

Ruth Snyder, in a blue robe, stands in a corner while her lover, Judd Gray, delivers the first murderous blow to the head of her sleeping husband, Albert, in 1927 (Ruth would later finish the job). The immense physical distance between the lovers, both of whom gaze straightforward rather than at the victim, may presage the emotional distance that would follow when the couple turned on each another in court. The scene is framed by a waist-high wooden banister, not unlike that of a witness or jury box, over which Albert Snyder gazes beseechingly at the museum visitors.

Richard Speck is shown with his hands outstretched above the neck of a bound-and-gagged nurse in uniform, one of the eight that Speck would brutalize in a 1966 dormitory killing spree. In the Musée, Speck appears lean and clean-cut, light reflecting off his smooth, hairless hands. Invisible is the "Born to Raise Hell" tattoo on his sweater-covered arm. Speck's gaze is placid, directed into the empty space above the nurse, his head eerily framed by the reflection of a metallic picture frame on the wall.

Vacated of the violent movements and passions that define primal acts, the figures in the Wax Musée seem battle weary and burdened by their psychic demons. John Christie, "The Full Moon Strangler" from Nottinghill, London (page 101), stands over a woman in a negligee, a rope taut around her neck. Christie, who killed at least seven women in the 1940s and '50s, apparently gassed and strangled his victims while sexually assaulting them. In this scene, however, he appears tired and distracted, seemingly unaware that he is missing his right hand. In another exhibit, an unidentified women in saddle shoes looks impassively at her fingernails while being bludgeoned over the head by a young man (John Roche, "The Rape Killer"), a trompe l'oeil cement-block hallway stretching into the distance behind them (page 100). The Wax Musée offers us a chamber of criminal horrors culled from across the decades, but in their static, timeworn banality, these primal scenes become at once approachable and discomforting.

Santangelo positioned her museum with an educational mission: "a wax show teaches the good things in life and also teaches that crime doesn't pay. What makes a person bad? What makes a clock tick, bad or good?"[8] That said, the lessons to be learned here are as complex and ambiguous as the questions posed. "Good" within the wax museum is often equally tainted by anxiety and horror. Beside the celebrities and murderers, the Musée featured the products of famous births. Some of these births were the subject of much celebration and publicity, such as the Dionne Quintuplets born in Ontario, Canada, in 1934. Yet much as the lives of the real Dionne sisters were marred by exploitation and tragedy, the wax quints seem to have suffered from separation and neglect. Three of the wax infants are pictured, stacked in hermetic glass cubes, their missing sisters unaccounted for.[9] A two-headed baby struggles beneath the piercing stare of its doctor, its precious few moments of life forever suspended and put on display. Most unsettling is the large display devoted to Lina Medina, the five-year-old Peruvian mother (pages 102–103). Medina became an international sensation in 1939 when her mother brought her to a hospital with a suspected tumor and doctors found that the child was eight months pregnant. The father of the infant was never identified, although Medina and her child were brought to the U.S. for study.[10] In her wax incarnation, Medina lies dwarfed within a hospital bed, her arms pinned at her sides, staring at the ceiling. A nurse holding Medina's infant keeps a watchful eye, yet the overall mood of the setting is of isolation and unspoken trauma.

I am not certain that Freud would have found the lessons of the Wax Musée to have been particularly clear or effective. What we find here are primal scenes that are immobilized, cleansed of the action, rage, and sound that would give them their tremendous power to wreak devastation within the "real" world. But in the process, this freezing process creates room for uncertainty and ambivalence. Our point of identification shifts and loses focus as it reflects off the surface of the static wax faces. Much as with a live primal encounter, our own position, and our moral clarity, is shattered when confronted with a scene that defies comprehension. Unlike a true primal scene, however, Santangelo's museum allows us to revisit, again and again, enshrined icons to those events that haunt us. The continued popularity of displays that have outlived the real-life interest in the events they depict serves as a testament to Coney Island's compulsion to repeat. "Only God makes the man," Santangelo once stated, "but man makes copies."[11] The wax museum is a site for eternal return, the continual replaying of trauma, much like the child that ceaselessly reenacts the departure of her mother, soothing herself by making a game out of that which she finds most terrifying.

AFTERIMAGES

Perhaps even more haunting than the commercial exhibits at Coney Island are the afterimages that "regular folk" left behind, those pictorial traces of their own idiosyncrasies, perversions, and tics. These traces are particularly prevalent among the staged studio photographs that surface within the archives of the Coney Island Museum or appear for sale in flea markets and online auctions. The relations between those pictured in these images, orphaned and displaced from their original settings, come unhinged. Most of the photographs are of couples and families, but the clichéd settings and standardized props do little to universalize or even to normalize the relationships they depict. While some of the awkwardness can be attributed to historical shifts in portraiture styles, in many of the images there is an excess of tension and affect that remains palpable, if not amplified by temporal distance.

Some images have become inscrutable with the passage of time. In a 1942 image, two women are photographed with their heads poking through a painted cutout. The bodies depicted are of nude women posing for the camera beneath suggestive lines of text: "I'm so little but so dependable"; "You must come up and see me sometime." The famous Mae West line suggests that these figures might reference famous actresses or burlesque stars. There is little evidence in the rendering of the bodies or hairstyles, however, to suggest individual characters. Moreover, the image is rife with visual contradictions that thwart interpretation. The nude female bodies combine ample breasts, bellies, and thighs with muscular shoulders, buttocks, and necks, implying more than a hint of masculinity (an effect that is heightened by the countenances of the particular women captured here).

The settings for most studio photographs at Coney Island were far less titillating. Backdrops would often consist of popular modes of transportation (cars, trains, or boats), festooned with Coney Island flags, in which visitors would pose with their friends and family. Some patrons posed informally, while many others approached the studio shots with the utmost gravity, standing stony faced before the camera. A few of the backdrops expanded into even more loaded generic territory. A large number of recovered studio photographs position patrons around an imaginary bar, complete with glasses and painted liquor bottles. As visitors feign drunkenness, sit awkwardly beside their parents or spouses, or stare with sullen, expressionless faces before faux cocktails, one gets the uncanny sense that these simulated scenarios have been played out before.

Other shots innocently proffer a psychoanalytic, visual feast. The unconscious here is on full display, as in one studio photograph of a four-year-old boy and his mother. The child stands at the wheel of an open car, while his mother sits outside the vehicle, at some distance behind him,

Opposite: Souvenir photograph. "Ruth (me) and Louise Templeton (Mrs.), July 25th, 1942 (Saturday Night), Coney Island, N.Y."

Real Photo Postcard, 1928.

before a painted backdrop of a country road. The child's head is unusually large for his body. His slicked-down hair, collared shirt, and belt suggest a preternatural maturity, as does his stance, leaning authoritatively on the steering wheel. The flattened perspective of the photograph makes the mother appear smaller than her child; she smiles demurely with her hand in her lap beneath his towering figure. Mother and child, however, share a certain warmth of expression, a roundness of feature, and a symmetry in their matching, glistening, parted hair. The fantasy suggested by the photo-studio scenario, one of modernity, freedom, and technology, obscures a far older, and darker, wish—a souvenir of the Oedipal complex fulfilled.

Coney Island promises visitors a return to childhood, a reinvigoration of the desires and pleasures deeply buried within the adult. In many ways, it makes good on this pledge. Freud would perhaps caution us, however, to the presence of deeper, more insidious fantasies residing within the submerged dream life of the inner child. At the very least, we would do well to remain attuned to the symptoms and anxieties continually manifested in Coney Island's shifting displays. Alongside the exotic and the sensational, we may find that our interest in even the most outlandish of enticements is rooted uncomfortably close to home.

Notes

1. See Georges Didi-Huberman, *Invention of Hysteria: Charcot and the Photographic Iconography of the Salpêtrière*, trans. Alisa Hartz (Cambridge, MA: MIT Press, 2004).

2. Scott Webel, *"Kinderbrutanstalt*: Leisure Space and the Coney Island Baby Incubators," *Text, Practice, Performance* 5 (2003): 9. According to Geoffrey T. Hellman, the location of the exhibits in Coney Island might have had additional unforeseen benefits: "one lady, expectant, took a ride on a roller-coaster, had her baby prematurely, and was not more than a block away from an incubator. Pretty handy!" From "Dr. Couney's Babies," *The New Yorker* (July 6, 1929): 10.

3. See Danielle Knafo and Kenneth Feiner, *Unconscious Fantasies and the Relational World* (New York: Routledge, 2005), 31–56.

4. As quoted in Roberta Leviton, "Cardboard Paradise: The Story of Coney Island," unpublished manuscript, Archives and Special Collections Division, Brooklyn College, CUNY, p. 28. Some reports cite the demise of the Eden Musée in a 1928 fire, although references to the attraction continue into the early 1930s. See Michael Immerso, *Coney Island: The People's Playground* (New Brunswick, NJ: Rutgers, 2002), 135.

5. E. B. White, "Coney," *The New Yorker* (July 11, 1931): 13. White visited the Eden Musée on this trip.

6. Cecilia Rasmussen, "Girl's Grisly Killing Had City Residents Up in Arms," *Los Angeles Times* (February 4, 2001): B3.

7. "'This Is Going to Get Interesting Before It's Over': Notes on W. E. Hickman's Trial and 'Confessions,'" unpublished manuscript and scrapbook, Archives of the Coney Island Amateur Psychoanalytic Society. Philosopher and novelist Ayn Rand was apparently intrigued by Hickman's case, favorably adopting one of his defense statements, "What is good for me is right." See Scott Ryan, *Objectivism and the Corruption of Rationality: A Critique of Ayn Rand's Epistemology* (Lincoln, NE: Writers Club Press, 2003), 337.

8. From an unpublished interview with Santangelo conducted by Dick Zigun, ca. 1981. Notes held in the archives of the Coney Island Museum.

9. Handwritten notes in the Coney Island Museum archive indicate that the head of a Dionne quint was located in storage in 1981 (along with Abraham Lincoln, Mussolini, Hitler, Frank Sinatra, two James Deans, and Martha Beck, "lesbian killer").

10. "Mother, 5, to Visit Here: Peruvian Child and Her Son to Be Guests of Chicago Doctors," *New York Times*, August 8, 1940.

11. Dick Zigun interview, Coney Island Museum.

Fred and Donald surveying the Trump domain in Coney Island, circa 1973.

ACKNOWLEDGMENTS

Thanks go first and foremost to Aaron Beebe, director of the Coney Island Museum, for his invitation to create an exhibition celebrating the centennial of Freud's visit to Coney Island. With great enthusiasm he put the museum's resources at my disposal. His knowledge and encouragement were invaluable. I owe this book to the generosity of Christine Burgin. Her wonderful ideas truly brought it to life. She is not only my publisher but fully a coeditor. I want to thank Amy Herzog, Aaron Beebe, and Norman Klein for their essays. Indeed it was Norman Klein's essay "Freud in Coney Island" that inspired us to create a show in the first place. I was delighted that Laura Lindgren agreed to design the book. Her work is beautiful. Don Kennison's expert reading of the text at the eleventh hour is greatly appreciated.

Thanks to Sheelah Bevan at the Museum of Modern Art, the librarians at the New-York Historical Society, and Ingrid Shaffner for taking time to help with my research. Frank Maresca and Elenore Weber from the Ricco/Maresca Gallery generously allowed us to reproduce drawings from the Fredrich Fried archive. Costa Mantis's photographs of The World in Wax Musée enhance this book's pages. Thanks also to the Die Keure printers, Marilyn Kushner, and Annette Leddy.

Of course this project would not have been possible but for the members of the Coney Island Amateur Psychoanalytic Society themselves. Thanks to Robert Troutman for rescuing the archive and sharing his memories and to Bob Rosenzweig and Patricia White for their contributions.

The DVD was made possible by Sal Mallimo's very knowledgeable work on the titles and the expertise of Colorlab restoring the films and transferring them to video. Thanks, too, to Frances Parsons for her work on the soundtrack of *The Lonely Chicken Dream*. Funding was provided by a grant from New York State Council on the Arts.

As always I could not have created the exhibition without my husband, Eric Muzzy, whose inventiveness and artistic sensibility played an essential role. I should mention in particular his meticulous re-creation of the working model of Albert Grass's Dreamland.

Opposite: Fred Trump bought Steeplechase Park in 1965 with plans to destroy it. In 1966 Trump mailed out engraved invitations to a party on September 21 celebrating the demolition of Steeplechase. He offered bricks to guests to throw through the funny face painted on the windows. Bikini-clad models posed in a bulldozer's shovel for publicity photos. Demolition began the following day, and by January 1967 Steeplechase Park was just a memory.

CONTRIBUTORS

AARON BEEBE is an artist and museum professional with a background in the fine arts and preservation. He began a love affair with Coney Island as a consultant to the Coney Island Museum while working as the archivist for theater director Robert M. Wilson. He has equally wide-ranging and concentrated experience in various fields, including the restoration and conservation of gilded wooden artifacts, academic work in cultural studies, and his own career as a creator of mixed-media works on paper. Since 2003 his background in Anthropology and Art History as well as his own work as an artist have brought new directions to the Coney Island Museum. Under his supervision, Coney Island USA has expanded the museum's exhibitions and programming to include public forums at academic institutions, exhibitions of contemporary art for the community, and several new programs, including an updated "Ask the Experts" series and the new Art/Business Incubator.

ZOE BELOFF is an artist and Associate Professor at Queens College, CUNY, teaching in the departments of Media Studies and Art. She works with a range of cinematic imagery: film, stereoscopic projection performance, interactive media, and installation. Her projects are philosophical toys, objects to think with, investigating a space where technology intersects with unconscious desire. She is particularly adept at dreaming her way into the past. Zoe's work has been exhibited internationally. Venues include: The Whitney Museum, MoMA, The Freud Dream Museum, Pacific Film Archives, and the Pompidou Center. This is the second book she has edited in conjunction with Christine Burgin. The first, *The Somnambulists: A Compendium of Source Material*, was published in 2008.

AMY HERZOG is Coordinator of the Film Studies Program and Assistant Professor of Media Studies at Queens College, CUNY. Focusing on the intersections of philosophy and film theory, she has written extensively on the work of Gilles Deleuze in relation to popular media. Her current research involves the history of coin-operated pornographic peep show film machines. She has recently completed a book, *Dreams of Difference, Songs of the Same: The Musical Moment in Film*, forthcoming from the University of Minnesota Press.

"The Whirlpool," Steeplechase, Coney Island, 1938.

NORMAN KLEIN is a cultural critic, media historian, and novelist. His work concentrates on how consumer spectacle and confused urban planning hide social conditions. He has expanded these interests into two series of books, one on cultural histories of forgetting, another on the history of special-effects environments. Among his best-known work: *The History of Forgetting: Los Angeles and the Erasure of Memory, The Vatican to Vegas: The History of Special Effects, Freud in Coney Island and Other Tales,* and *Seven Minutes: The Life and Death of the American Animated Cartoon.* Currently, he is the author and co-director of a science-fiction interactive novel about how the twentieth century was imagined before it began (1893–1925). Entitled *The Imaginary Twentieth Century,* it recently opened at ZKM (The Center for the Arts and Media, in Karlsruhe, Germany), for a two-year run (until November 2009). Simultaneously, over the next five years, it will show in the U.S., Europe, and Asia (five exhibitions in 2008–2009). In fall 2009 *The Imaginary Twentieth Century* will be published as a book/DVD-ROM (Verso and ZKM), and in 2010 *Jumping Off the Half-Moon Hotel* (a novel set in Coney Island during the fifties). Klein is a professor at the California Institute of the Arts.

DREAMLAND

The Coney Island Amateur Psychoanalytic Society 1301 Surf Avenue Coney Island N.Y. Telephone CO 6-0466

September 21, 1930

Dear Mr. Edward F. Tilyou,

Enclosed please find a brief prospectus of DREAMLAND: its History and Purpose, Plans for the Future, the first amusement park ever devoted to the elucidation of dreams in accordance with the discoveries of Doctor Sigmund Freud M.D.

Now for the first time, the masters of our nightly perambulations, the "Psychic Censor", "Consciousness", the "Unconscious", the "Dreamwork" and the "Libido" will be assembled into pavilions, in a style both orderly and gay. A "Train of Thought" linking each funhouse, fueled in its endeavor by an an ample supply of ideas will be set in motion. Once established, DREAMLAND will grow to literally undreamed of proportions for the enlightenment of this and future generations.

The deep interest in the park by members of the Coney Island Amateur Psychoanalytic Society as well as other public-spirited citizens suggested that a permanent organization should be effected and in June 1929 a Board of Trustees as well as officers were elected. An application to the Board of Regents, University of the State of New York for a provisional educational charter was granted in the same year.

Now the groundwork is done. There are few uncertainties. The plans for the future are clearly outlined. It is in the light of these developments that the Trustees cordially extend an invitation to invest in our venture as chief underwriter of DREAMLAND.

I look forward to a long and profitable partnership.

Sincerely,

Albert Grass

Albert Grass

President pro tem

GEO. C. TILYOU'S
STEEPLECHASE PARK
CONEY ISLAND   NEW YORK

October 6th, 1930

Mr. Albert Grass,
1301 Surf Avenue, Coney Island

Dear Sir:

In reference to your letter of September
29th, I do not Believe that the public would
enjoy your medical attractions which appear to
cater to rather pruient tastes. I have never
heard of the foreign doctor whose name you
mention and I cannot imagine that the public
would find his ideas to their liking.

I must decline your offer.

Very truly yours.,

Edw Tilyou

Drawing for a child's carousel by William F. Mangels (1866–1958), W. F. Mangels Co. Carousell Works, Coney Island, ca. 1918–19.

Unless otherwise noted, all images are from the collection of The Coney Island Museum.
Pages 14–15, 128: courtesy of Ricco/Maresca Gallery, photographs by Ellen McDermott;
pages: 46–47, 57, 60, 63, 65, 70–78, 85–99, 126–27 Archive of the Coney Island Amateur Psychoanalytic Society;
page 54: courtesy of the New York City Department of Records;
page 81: courtesy Patricia White; page 83: courtesy of Bob Rosenzweig

The Coney Island Amateur Psychoanalytic Society and Its Circle
Edited by Zoe Beloff
2009

ISBN: 978-0-9778696-0-2

Book design and composition by Laura Lindgren
The text of this book is composed in Monotype Bell.
Printed by Die Keure, Belgium

Published by Christine Burgin
243 West 18th Street
New York, NY 10011
www.christineburgin.com